Postseason
"A Baseball Club for Girls?"

Caroline

"Have a great day," I hang up the phone, wiping tears off my eyes and grabbing a tissue from the table beside me. I cry into it more. My dad isn't here and the bus should be here in less than two minutes.

"Bye Mom!" I call running and retrieving my lunch and backpack at the same time. I make sure to wipe one final tear from my face before getting on the packed bus that is flooded with students for the first day of school.

I practically crawl into a seat ducking my head from the papers being thrown around all over the bus. The eighth and seventh graders are trying to be cool as the sixth graders try not to cry. I'm so nervous I'm sweating buckets and its cold out. It's at the most sixty degrees out and I'm wearing the ugliest sweater I promised my Grandma I'd wear. It's gross brown and stitched terribly. I don't know why my Grandma is still in knitting classes.

The tears spill over again when I hear my dad's words, 'have a great day', as if. My dad is across the country and there's less than a month until my birthday.

My dad is a sports announcer for Major League Baseball. He's on TV for the games and most of the time he goes on road trips with the team. Right now, he's all the way in Seattle and it's almost obvious that our team will make it to the playoffs so that means he won't be home in October, my birth month and October 15th, my birthday.

My mom calls Dad's job 'un-family friendly'. I can't agree more, I think its super cool to see Dad on TV and hear his voice, but it's nothing compared to talking to him in person.

This morning Dad called to talk to all of us. 'Us' being my brother and sisters, Cece is in ninth grade, Ashley is in third, and Cody is in first as of today, and I'm in sixth. Dad was nice when he talked to me, but you could tell that Mom gave him an earful already and he was kind of sick of it.

Alexandria Waters slides beside me and sets everything down. "Can I sit here?" she asks, it's an annoying question because she's already sitting right next to me. It's pointless, but I nod anyway.

Alexandria Waters is kind of annoying, but I guess she has a good reason to always be upset. Her family has kind of isolated her brother, who is a Major League Baseball player. I guess her parents don't like that he plays baseball, so they chose not to speak to him. I'm not sure on the whole back story, but I know she misses him a lot and that sometimes her parents act like she's their only kid.

I rerun the whole phone conversation with my dad again. He said that he would be home soon and that there was barley twenty games left. I was too scared to ask about my birthday, so I didn't, instead I decided that Mom probably knew and she said that that was up to him. If he decided to come home, awesome, but if not, I'd have a birthday alone.

She didn't say it exactly like that. "Caroline, I'm not sure." She actually said. "I'm sorry, but if Daddy is home for your birthday that will be just great, for everyone, but it's looking like he may have to work."

I didn't cry or anything when she said that. I just got quiet, which is something I do when I'm kind of torn between crying and screaming. My mom, Cece, Ashley, and Cody know this so they leave me alone when this happens.

As the bus pulls into the school parking lot, I stop thinking about that. Instead, I think about everyone who is probably about to go compare me to my sister. Cece made a big mark here. She was everyone's friend and all the teachers thought she was amazing. I get okay grades and my behavior is great, but nobody knows me and I'm horrible at Social Studies and Math.

I look at lot like Cece too. We're three years apart, she's in ninth grade and I'm in sixth. Cece has blonde hair and brown eyes and is medium height; I have strawberry blonde hair and blue eyes and am about an inch shorter than her. If you gave us the same eye color we are identical. We look just like Dad, but Ashley and Cody look more like Mom.

"Hey Cece," says someone and it occurs to me that people will probably think that Cece is still in the middle school. I guess not everyone knows what grade she's in now, not that I can blame them, I thought this morning that Cody was going into Kindergarten, he's in first grade.

"Um," I don't really say anything, I just run inside, along with everyone else. Mrs. Adams, Cece's old Science and Math teacher, stops me halfway in the hall and smiles.

"Cecelia Taylor, no way!" She says. I sigh. "Did you do something with your hair? I love it! Oh, I missed you so much!" She hugs me tight. I tug away.

"I'm her sister," I say. "Caroline Taylor, I'm in sixth grade. Cece is in ninth grade this year." Ms. Adams looks like I just punched her in the face. I've met Mrs. Adams lots of times, mostly when Cece was in sixth and seventh grade. Last year, Mrs. Adams co-thought with Mr. Adams as the drama teacher, they're married so they teach drama together. Cece was in the school play and she played the lead so I saw her a lot last year too.

"Another Taylor, that's awesome!" She shouts instead her face expression changing. "You know I had your sister every year she was here, that was how much my schedule was moved around."

"Ha," I mumble and force a smile. I knew that Cece had Mrs. Adams, Mr. Adams, and Ms. Tumble. Those were her favorites.

"Let me just tell you, if you are anything like Cecelia, you will be a terrific fit for this school." She tells me.

"Okay," I say. Great, Cece and I couldn't be more different. She has so many friends; I don't have many at all. She is smart, I'm okay. The list is endless.

"Have a good day and tell Cecelia I said hello." She walks away and starts talking to another group of kids. I have Mrs. Adams for science this year and Mr. Adams for math.

After a few classes, I make it to lunch with no one talking to me at all. This makes me wish that I was still in elementary school, with Ashley and Cody in the same building as me. Trying not to think about that, I turn my head to the eighth and seventh grade tables. Smiling and laughing while the sixth graders are holding their lunch to their chests, looking like they might puke.

"Cece!" cries a group of kids standing over me. "Why are you sitting here? Everyone wants you to sit over there! Did you do something with your hair?" The questions come flying at me as I duck my head into the table.

"I'm not Cece," I say quietly. "I'm Caroline, her sister."

"Yeah," snorts a girl. "And I'm Joanne the alien that is taking over this body!"

"Seriously," I snap. "Cece is in ninth grade!" My words come out chipped and stern. All of them look at me angrily.

"Whatever," says one of them. "You are nothing like your sister."

"You barely know me!" I cry, bursting into tears. "You don't have to be so mean, it's my first day!"

"Oh no," says a different one. "She's Cece Taylor's sister, maybe we should help her out."

"I don't need the pity," I mumble to myself.

"Sorry," says the one that was mean to me. "Tell Cece we say hi,"

I promise I will and the rest of the day drags on and annoys me like crazy. I want to go home and this day just gets longer and longer. The day ends with Mom picking me up and us going to get Cody and Ashley.

"My first day," sighs Cece. "was great!"

"Good for you sweetie," says Mom. "I'm so glad." She turns to me. "What about you, Caroline? How was your day?"

"Fine," I say in the voice I used for the girls at lunch.

"Doesn't sound 'fine', what happened?" Mom replies. I sigh and glare at Cece.

"Everyone thinks that I'm you!" I say, starting to tear up. "They think you just dyed your hair."

Cece fluffs her hair back and laughs. "Those dumb seventh graders, now eighth graders, they don't know anything. I would never dye this beauty." Cece is full of it.

Mom gives her a look and laughs. "Don't they know your grade?" I ask Cece.

Cece does another hair fluff and smiles. "I don't know." She says. She takes out her cell phone and begins to type away, smiling while doing so. "Oh my gosh," she gushes. "This was the best day, ever."

I look away as we get to the elementary school. Right now, I wish I were there, where nobody compared me to Cece, well at least not as much.

"I set a play date up for you, Caroline." My mother says and I cringe. Play dates are for babies and I am not a baby. I've tried to explain to my mom about this, but she said that I need more friends. Of course this is because of Cece having the whole student body as friends.

"Ha," snorts Cece. "Mom Kayla and Marcy are coming over, k?" My mother smiles and nods like she pretty much always does when Cece says something. She could say that she was going to rob a bank and my mom would just nod and smile like always.

"Do you know Jacqueline Heaters?" Mom asks. "Her Grandma owns a foster home in their house. It's a beautiful service and Ruth says that Jackie might use a few friends as well."

"Ruth Keener?" wonders Cece. "She used to work at the elementary school. She's so great with kids! Didn't her daughter just die?"

"Yup," Mom's voice turns dark and sad. "Maggie Keener-Heaters was her name. That's why Ms. Keener has a foster home, because that's what Maggie would have wanted. David, Jackie's father, just moved to San Diego for his job. Ruth is watching Jackie."

"I don't want to be friends with someone sad and lonely!" I cry. I've heard of Jackie Heaters and she's miserable. She has about twenty foster siblings, some from India, France, and Switzerland. Everywhere, and her mom just passed away, her life isn't fair. I don't want to hear her whine or anything.

"Caroline Taylor, please!" Mom screams. "You will be her friend. You can't imagine someone with that many kids in her home to be happy."

"She's right, Caroline." Cece says. "She sounds nice and besides, won't it be nice to know someone in Middle School?"

"Shut up," I mumble. Cece has had friends since the day she was born, I however, have just about zero.

"Mommy, Mommy!" voices appear from the front of our car. It's Ashley and Cody yelling to let them in. We open the door and they start overflowing with bubbles. "I am so happy," I hear Ashley say to Cece. Easy for her to say, nobody set her up with a play date.

Unlike her, I did.

And also unlike her, I don't have my dad on my birthday.

I hate Middle School already.

Alex

I look around my hands crossed in my lap as I sprawl on the floor dancing to the song playing on the stereo. If it wasn't for the eight years of dance lessons there's no way I would be able to do the splits in front of everyone and dance to this ridiculous song, but I am.

Everyone claps as our dance ends and I run back to the school locker room to change for the next number. I'm at my dance competition and only my brother's girlfriend is here to watch me. I guess that means I'm pretty pathetic, but she was glad to help out since my brother is a professional baseball player and was busy this weekend. My parents on the other hand just hate dancing in general and think I should go to career classes every Saturday morning.

"That was great girls," says Coach Linda from the other side of the room. "But I think that we can do better if we work a little bit harder. That dance got us second place!" We cheer and she gets us up top for the next number. I sigh, if only my brother could see this.

The music starts and we all form into a line until we do the 'play dead' move I find very stupid. After that some do spins while others like me do handstands walking through them. There's no doubt this dance is harder than any other and all together it looks amazing, but it all depends if we do this right.

At the end we jump and a few of us fly on to the pyramid of girls, ending our littlest in splits in the center. As the crowd cheers, I wobble off the top of one of the three pyramids and fall to the ground. I'm not hurt, so I make up for the mistake my doing turns and spins and posing. The crowd loves it, but my ankle is sore.

"Alex," Coach Linda grabs my arm. "What happened?" Gwen Biggley, another girl in my dance class crosses her arms and points at me.

"She ruins everything!" Gwen screams. "I'm sure we're going to so lose now, thanks a lot. This was everything to me and now it's ruined! Spotlight stealer!"

I groan. Gwen Biggley is the meanest girl in my grade and she won't hold back for anything. I'm just happy she's going to quit soon to be on the Spirit Dancing Pon Pom team at school. That should make everything easier. "I slipped." I explain. "I didn't mean to fall; I thought I made up for it."

"Whatever," Gwen says. She shoves me out of her way as she changes into her sweatpants and t-shirt.

"It's fine," Coach Linda says. "I think we did pretty well, but I don't know so don't think that we're just magically going to win." She crosses her fingers as we head upstairs to do the final number with the other teams. It's the sweatpants chillax dance, as Coach Linda calls it. It's a really funny dance that we all learned at separate times and never practiced with the other teams.

My team files out and dances to the first verse while the team from Washers does the same thing, only backwards so it all fits it together. The crowd is on their feet dancing to the song too, all of the teams bow and await the results.

"I bet we won," I hear someone from Washers say. Washers is kind of a rich town and they get really good coaches each year and always get first, second, or third place. Last year they placed fifth, but that was because of budget cuts in the area.

"Second place," says the announcer. "Riverside Waters Dance Squad." That's us. We lost, but they reward us with trophies and our badges from joining the team. The Washers get first and they cheer like crazy and get to do their dance one last time. I try and find Angela, my brother's girlfriend, in the crowd with the rest of the parents.

I'm quiet as we walk to her car. I clutch my trophy in my hand and throw my dance bag in the trunk. "I don't care what anyone says," She tells me. "You did awesome, I'm taking you to Julio's for lunch," I smile. Julio's is this modern day restaurant forced to look like a kitchen and their food is the best ever.

"That fall was pretty scary," Angela looks at my ankle that I now realize is kind of swollen. "Are you sure that you're okay?"

"Yeah," I say. "My coach and Gwen Biggley thought I was stealing the whole dance, but I didn't want to just cry with everyone watching. I know it was pathetic." I start to tear up.

"What's wrong?" Angela asks. I wipe my tears. I could say that someone I barely know is the one taking me to dance competitions not my mom or my dad or anyone close to me. I feel like nothing and nobody realizes it and if I injured my ankle my mom will drag me out of dance forever.

As we arrive at Julio's I limp to my seat, but don't let Angela notice. I order my favorite Tacos with a side of the fresh salsa and fries and Angela doesn't even hesitate with Julio's dessert. We both share this giant brownie ice cream thing.

"Okay," She says as we finish eating. "Your mom called and wants me to bring you home soon, but I think we need to go to Urgent Care real quick because your ankle looks awful."

I sigh. My ankle does look pretty bad and my hand hurts too. I struggle to the car as we go into Urgent Care. Apparently I have a fever also and I can't even strain Angela a smile in the waiting room. She looks at my leg and arm and smiles. "I'm sure it's just a bruise," She says.

But it's not just a bruise.

"I think her ankle is fractured," The doctor says, he can tell I'm disappointed with the results so he shows me how it looks. "See, it's going to be okay, the swelling went down. The fall just twisted it a little."

"Are crutches in the question?" Angela asks, I can tell she doesn't want me to have to go through much pain. I'm just scared about dancing again. Mom and Dad are going to get mad enough as it is.

"Um, yes, but only for a short period of time. I don't think she'll be able to walk well without them and about her arm, it's a little sprained she may want to put some ice on it." He explains.

"Thank you, very much." Angela says.

As we get home, Angela goes to the front door before me to explain the problem to my parents, who aren't happy with my crutches and ice pack.

"Her ankle and arm are sprained." Angela tells them. "She, um, uh, did some awesome dance moves and they said it was just from the dancing, she'll be fine."

My mom shoots Angela a devil look. Mom hates all of my brother's girlfriends, that's because she hates my brother. Mom hates everyone and eyes Angela carefully. "Okay then," Mom doesn't blink. "Goodbye." She shuts the door on Angela before I can say thank you.

"I can't believe this," Mom slams the door she calls for my dad as they take a look at my ankle and hand. "How dare she just think it's okay?" Mom has Dad carry me to my bed and they make me nap for two hours before I can do anything. I don't argue because my parents hate that.

17

I set my crutches against my bedside table and lay my leg on the ice bag that my mom and dad set up on the end of the bed. I sigh as my dad and mom argue about the dangers of my ankle and arm. I can't help but want to scream at them that it's not a big deal. I've sprained my hand before, which is probably why it sprained so easily. My ankle I've sprained before, but never broke. It doesn't matter, though. I'm fine.

"Get some rest now," Dad tells me. "If you need anything just use the kitchen phone." The kitchen phone is one of the many numbers my parents connected each of the room landlines to so we can reach each other throughout the house like an intercom.

"Ok," I say back smiling. I'm trying to not let the everlasting pain in my right ankle show. I work so hard at my dancing and if I say that my ankle hurts, Mom will pull me out so fast I won't have time to say no.

After they leave my bedside table phone starts ringing. I reach over with my hand that isn't sprained and pick it up. "Hello?"

"Hey, Al, it's Al." It's my brother, Alexander. My parents think that we'll both go by our name

'Alexandria' and 'Alexander', but we both like to be called Alex and Al and stuff. I smile when I hear my brother's voice. I haven't seen him all summer.

"Oh hi," I say into the phone. I'm not exactly thrilled when I say hi. I guess it's us losing and my stupid ankle.

"Listen, Ally, I just want you to know that I wish I could come home sooner, but I'll be here as soon as possible." He says. I stop him halfway.

He loves his job and it isn't fair for him to come home for me. He loves playing baseball. "No," I say. "You stay and come home for Christmas like you planned, I swear I'm fine."

"But what about Mom and Dad? Are they driving you crazy yet?" I snort. OF COURSE! They say that he is a brat and that he needs to come home at least ten times a day, but I want my brother to be happy.

"I'm fine, and I want you to come home at Christmas, like I said! Please, please, please!" I beg. His laugh comes out like its millions and hundreds miles away, and it shouldn't.

I hear footsteps come up the stairs and say goodbye quickly before Alex can say anything either. I miss my brother so much and because of baseball he can't come home. He isn't invited and probably never will be.

"Alexandria," My dad walks into my room. He has a clouded expression on his face and he looks at me like I've committed a crime. "Please rest, you have a hurt ankle."

"Okay Daddy," I say blowing him a kiss. He smiles back and hands me a sheet of papers that have building and career projects for my school.

"Your mom and I are going to be at the Middle School this week taping some videos for the school board meeting on October 15th," He tells me. "You and some friends can be in them, but I need their names by Thursday."

I sigh. I don't want to be in videos for the school board and besides what friends? My biggest idea of a friend right now is myself and even I let myself down today breaking my ankle. I ruined any chance at a solo in the next dance routine.

For a second I think about writing some random names down, names that will get people mad for ever being volunteered to be in such a video. "Okay, daddy, but what's the video about?"

"Educational Safety," He says.

"Oh," I whisper in a low voice.

"And," He adds. "If you're well enough, I thought maybe you and your friends could make a dance video too, making educational safety more fun, you know?"

"Yeah," I mumble. A dance video for the school board to see? I don't know, but it seems fun, but I don't know what 'fun' means when it comes to executives from the school board.

I decide to sleep on it and get some rest instead. I can worry about some dumb dance videos and educational safety in the morning.

***

"How pathetic," Gwen Biggley trips me on my crutches. I fall to the ground, but not before John Anderson helps me up and shoots Gwen a glare. "You aren't hurt at all," She whispers into my ear.

I ignore her and walk into school. "Let's go, Spirit and Fight, We can win with you on our side!" The high school cheerleaders and some eighth grade ones cheer in the main lobby. "Tryouts are all week and we hope you can come," says Cece Taylor handing me a flyer.

"No thanks," I give it back to her. She hands it back to me.

"No, really," She says. "I would so consider it! I was at competition on Saturday for the upper dance class and I saw you guys perform, it was amazing! You have to at least GO to tryouts, please!"

"I don't know," I reply in a shy voice. I'm not the cheeriest person at school and Cece Taylor is, unlike her sister Caroline who never talks to anyone.

"Consider it, please; I think you'll love it."

"I'll come!" shouts spirited Rosie Dawkins. Her mom is like some French actress, but nobody knows who she is. I think I know who she is, Adelynn Simone Dawkins I think. She was in a move I watched once, but nobody else really thinks she exists and even if, her last name appears as Simone on TV so Rosie could be lying.

"Oh ok," Cece says unenthusiastically.

I feel bad for Rosie Dawkins and all for having a mom that lives in France and a dad who misses her very much, I mean she's probably really lonely, but she's still annoying and sometimes crazy. "When is it?" She asks.

"Take a flyer," demands Cece. Cece Taylor isn't mean, but when Rosie (who is a little bit of a dumb blonde) comes in and tries to act cool, you can't just stay magically calm.

Rosie looks over at the table and walks away without taking a flyer, instead she walks over to the spirit pon pom dancing station and talks to Julie Biggley, Gwen Biggley's sister, the head of that.

"You like to dance?" I ask her. Maybe my educational safety dance video can piece itself together without my help. She shrugs her shoulders and does a little high kick and smile, the full cheerleader type attitude, not a dancer.

"Sometimes I dance," She shrugs.

"Well, I have to make a dance video for the school board and was wondering if you'd be interested." Rosie tries not to look excited, but she is and I can tell. She smiles a big smile and takes the piece of paper I got out of my backpack from me.

"I guess I wouldn't mind it," She says.

"Okay whatever," I say and walk back to the dance table.

First and second hours were canceled because of the high school showing off the middle school extra circular activities. Since I'm using my crutches, I sit on the bleachers in the gym and work on a song to dance to for the video. Recently, I've discovered I really like to sing so I've been trying to write songs. I'm horrible, of course, but I feel like it's just trying that counts, plus it's not like anyone can hear my songs being sung.

Even if this video makes the school board happy, what about me and my dancing and ankle? And what about my brother coming home after the seasons over, how do I predict that? Whatever happens, I'm not sure that I'll ever know.

Rosie

I fall out of bed again my dark black hair is bed head and only a few minutes to spare before I have to be at school. With boxes packed and some not packed I can barely make my way around the house anymore.

I guess I'm moving, but I will never know. My mom, Adelynn Simone Dawkins, is a famous French actress who lives in Paris. I miss her a lot and haven't seen her in years. My dad says that a tea shop in Paris that is run by my grandparents isn't doing well and Mom wants us to move there and help while she continues her acting. We've been supposed to go since June and July, but now it's September and my dad is saying October. We don't have plane tickets yet.

The thing is, we don't have the money for plane tickets and Mom keeps offering to pay for them. My dad won't let her, though. He wants her to stay what she's doing and not worry about the money we don't have, but that's not true. My dad would do anything to get to Paris and be with my mom at this second and I know it. In a way, I really want to be in Paris too. I want to see the lights, the celebrities, the movies, and of course, my mom.

But if I'll ever get there, it will be sometime when I'm eighty at this point. Unless I develop a magical talent for acting and song like my mom, but right now I stink on ice.

"Ready Rosie?" asks my dad from downstairs. My dad drives me to school and most of the time I just walk home. The bus is too much for me. I live, breathe, and just about love everything thing about clothes and sparkles. I can't imagine life without glitter, that's one thing I hate about my mom being in Paris. No one to discuss hair, makeup, or boys with.

"Hey!" I shout walking down the stairs. "It's Friday, Sundae." Sundae is my French poodle. She's the most adorable thing in the world. I got her sixth months ago when my dad said we might be moving. He wanted me to have something to keep me company so he got me a 'French' poodle. Sundae is only nine months and is a baby French poodle, meaning she's small. When my dad is having private talks with my mom and I want something, she's the one I talk to.

"Yes, finally Friday." My dad mumbles walking into the kitchen. My dad owns a store in town; it's like a Technology Lab, only it's huge and full of computers, laptops, cell phones and more. I love it so much and I'm going to miss it when we move.

"September 10th, right?" I wonder. Most of the time I don't know what the day or date is. Lately people have been referring to me as a 'dumb blonde' and I guess I am, but I have super dark hair that Gwen Biggley insists on being dyed.

"Yup," My dad says. We get into the car and drive off. I haven't gotten used to Middle School yet, but my dad says I'll catch on. It's only a few days into school and I've realized how hard it can really be. I have a test next week on something I barely know, the only good thing is that I'm on Spirit Dance Pom Pom, which means I'm cooler that the cheerleaders.

Thinking about Spirit Pom Pom gives me something to glow about as I walk into school. Our first practice was last week and I really think that this is for me. In elementary school I was one of those small, little cheerleaders who never REALLY got to cheer at halftime and for a second I wanted to be one this year too, but then I realized that I might never get a chance to dance or do what I love without just doing Spirit Dance Pom Pom, which I love now.

"Good morning, Miss Rosie Dawkins," says Julie Biggley, she's in eighth grade and in charge or Spirit Dance Pom Pom. She might be related to snotty Gwen, but she's a good teacher for dance and is nice to most of the sixth graders, except for the rest of the world, then she's like her sister.

"Hey Julie," I reply and she laughs. I'm fake compared to some of these girls who think they're constantly on a reality show.

"Well, my oh my, nice to see you this fine morning, Rosie." Mrs. Adams waves to me. She's my Math teacher and is so nice. She always says something nice to me when I walk in her door.

My eyes are wide open when I look at the assignment on the white board. Math is actually really easy and fun in Mrs. Adams class. She does so many weird, quirky, and interesting assignments, but this one looks like it's going to be crazier than normal. We have to write a paper including math problems, but it has to be in the form of a movie summary.

"How am I supposed to do that?" Gwen Biggley cries from across the room. "This is stupid; I wish you didn't have to take math." I roll my eyes. Gwen

28

hates everything she has to actually put some effort into before passing.

"Oh, Genevieve, please stop complaining, I find it fun to mix subjects. When I was an English teacher my students would laugh when I would say write a paper with a scientific math problem telling a story about an event in Social Studies." Everyone laughs except Gwen who ignores Mrs. Adams and starts to write in bright pink pen on her paper.

I finish the day without homework and walk home expecting to see another box unpacked or packed up depending on the progress my dad's savings has made. I stumble across the front school lawn as the boy's baseball practice has begun and am intrigued to watch for some reason. Sports are kind of been a big blur to me. I don't understand how sports work. I've never had an interest, but baseball looks abnormal. As if I might want to play, but I have no idea how much better I would because with me it'd be impossible.

"Oh, hi, Rosie, how are you?" Jackson Spicer asks. Jackson used to be in my fifth grade class last year and is incredibly nice. I'm not going to tell him that I'm sitting here trying to learn about baseball by watching a little league team. I probably won't learn much, but I want to try it out. I pull out my phone and text my dad that I'll be late and he says okay.

"I'm okay," I reply. "Um, is it okay if I watch you guys practice?" I'm really shy and I'm not sure what the coaches will say about me watching their practice. I know my Spirit Pon Pom dancing coach is always upset about other dance and cheer teams watching us, she thinks that they'll find our weak spots or copy parts of our routines.

"Yeah, that's fine." Jackson answers. "I never imagined you liking baseball, Rosie."

I laugh. "Neither did I, I just thought I'd try it out, watching I mean." I smile and take a seat on the outside bleachers as they split into two teams for the practice. I immediately start to feel stupid when I watch them take positions. I don't know any of the names of the positions, I don't know what strikes, balls, or a home run is. I've heard of a base hit before, but maybe that's because it has the word 'base' in it like baseball. Other than that, I'm drawing blanks to everything.

Jacqueline Heaters takes the field too, which surprises me. This is a boy little league team, not a girls one.

"Is Jackie on your team?" I ask him, curious.

"Oh Jackie, oh nope, she just practices with us because one of our guys has a dislocated shoulder. You can play too." I make my face smile bright as the sun, but I couldn't play any baseball if the world depended on it.

"Um, I'm not sure how to play, yet. That's why I wanted to uh, watch." I say.

"Rosie, it's very simple." Jackson laughs. "Just join us, you can play shortstop." I nod and as he walks away my smile falters. I don't know what that means.

"In the middle of third base and second base," Jackie says heading towards third. I nod and sit down on the dirt ground getting up when I feel the dirt on my butt. "You have to stand," She demands and I do, but start to get uncomfortable. What if the ball is hit to me and I have to do something with it? Is the ball even allowed to be hit at people?

Scrambling the coach asks Jackie and me to leave the field. "Sorry gals, normally I would allow it, but we've got a postseason coming up and need some extra practice." Jackie and I head away from the field and my nervousness goes away, I never wanted to play, I just wanted to watch.

"Hey," Jackie says. "If you still want to try baseball out, I can show you a place to practice." Jackie Heaters is really nice. She lives in a foster home with her grandmother and a bunch of foster children and always appears sporty, but she's really girly too. She was on the cheer squad in elementary school too, but now she spends her time doing other activities like sports and helping her grandma and dad out. She's nice, but kind of bratty and snotty. She is always fixing her long blonde curls and she yells at the girls like Gwen sometimes, when she could be just like them. Only she isn't as mean as Gwen Biggley, not at all.

"I'm actually supposed to be heading home now," I tell her. "But thanks, I just wanted to see how to play." She snorts and I glare. "I know, I know, I sound stupid, but training me would take private lessons."

"That's a cool idea," She replies. "Private lessons, or like a club, right?" I nod. "I wouldn't think you would want that, but I guess I'm wrong."

"What's wrong with me?" I snap.

"You're just such a snotty cheerleader and don't you do that POM thing?"

"What's wrong with that?" I snap once more, my pale face getting red.

"Nothing, it's just well, kind of dumb. I liked cheer, remember, but now that's not cool and I like baseball, I wish there was like…" her voice trails off.

"A baseball club for girls?" I ask. Her face glows and she brightens up.

"EXACTLY!" She screams. "I bet if I had the chance, I could show those boys HOW to hit like a girl." I laugh. I was just joking with the club thing, but if she was serious it may not be a bad idea. I need more activities to do, at least before I move and I've never been in a team sport. Spirit Pon Pom is more like you do the best you can do, not the whole team like dance, cheer, or well, baseball.

"I guess it sounds alright, but I would stink."

"So would I," She laughs, her voice turning more preppy and fun. "I pretend to be good, so I don't go home right away with all the kids, but I'm not. I'd love to learn more."

"I would too," I say.

"Then why don't we do something?" Jackie wonders, sitting down on the bleachers again. "I would so love to be on baseball team where you can actually train and not just go out and stink."

"Maybe we can," I think out loud. "We just need someone, someone who's devoted to help us, and others out. The people who really want it to, a, a baseball club for girls."

***

"Hey Rosie," Dad says as I walk into the door. My dad is making his famous pepper pizza, homemade from his secret family recipe. I smile and set my things down. "What were you up to?"

"I was watching the boys at school play baseball," I answer. "I want to learn more about it, but I'm so confused when it comes to it, I think I'll just stick to Spirit Dance Pom Pom stuff, I'm not so good at everything else."

"I think you are," He replies setting out the plates for him and me. I smile. "I talked to Mom today; she says her filming is going great."

"That's great," I say, rolling my eyes. It doesn't matter what my mom is doing right now, she's always on the set of a movie and it always is 'going great' if it was going so great she would invite us to one of the premieres once in a while.

Dad says he doesn't want to be famous, he loves his job, and I do too, but being famous would be so cool. I guess he'd rather hide in the shadows that walk a mile in Mom's shoes. She's always on TV and he just wants to stay home and watch TV. If I had the choice, I don't know what I'd choose. I'm not talented enough to be on TV, but would I always want to be in the background? I'm not sure, and I'm glad that I don't have to choose my occupation right now.

"How's dinner?" He asks. I nod my face full of satisfaction. My dad makes the best pepper pizza.

"It's great!" I tell him. I clear my plate when I'm finished and go upstairs to check the Paris fundraiser savings. We're up to about one hundred and fifty, but that's still not enough for two tickets to Paris and all the things to do. My dad will have to get a job when we're there because my mom can't always supply the money for us. Like other famous celebrities, she'll be forced into giving most of her money to charity, which is fine, but we need money for food and our home and everything in between and then there's my school and education and extra after school activities.

I hurry out of my dad's office and into my bedroom to finish up my homework and get my stuff ready for practice tomorrow. Before going to sleep, I take out the picture of my mom and me from when I was four. That was the last time she was in the United States to visit us. She's been here since, but not here and she hasn't seen me in person since then either.

I've emailed her and watched her on television, even though I don't understand any of the French movies that she's been in, but I still love watching them.

Everyone says I look a lot like my dad and I do. I have glasses that I have to wear sometimes but I avoid them because they make look like a geek and with those on, I'm the perfect version of my dad only a girl. I may look like him, but looking at this picture I look a lot like my Mom too. She has the same long black hair as me and is always smiling with her eyes wide open.

I wish I could go to Paris right now.

Jackie

Rak and Jamal run from under my bed and scream in panic as I chase them away. Shutting the door behind them, I sigh and jump back onto my bed. I wanted to get my homework done, but with siblings popping up there and in there I might as well just give up.

Rak and Jamal are the six year old boys from India that our home cares for. They are nice, but they are just as mischievous and sneaky as any other first grade boys. My grandma wants them to be adopted by the same family, but right now that's a big low chance. We had two girls a few months ago and we still have one of them. Some families only want one kid, no matter how badly their twin may want them.

I have some many foster siblings it's not funny. The only good thing is I'm not a foster child myself. My grandparents own the home and I live with her because my dad lives in San Diego, where he works. My mom just passed away, so my dad got his old job back and is hoping to find a job here in Michigan, but for now he's working there and I guess he's okay with it.

My grandma and grandpa run this place and are really good with it too. The Maggie Keener-Heaters Forster Home has only been around for a few months, but the original "Keener Foster Home" has been around for longer. My grandparents decided to change the name in honor of my mom.

You'd be surprised how long we've had some of these kids. Not many get adopted and many parents who say they're going to adopt drop out, leaving the kids sad.

The doorbell rings and I hurry to answer it. Caroline Taylor walks into the door, her expression the same, sad looking face as always. I suppose her reason is as good as my sad face. Her dad won't be home in time for her birthday. Neither will mine, but at least hers has a choice. My dad has to work in January, which is when my birthday is, but her dad can come home anytime, he just chose to announce the games that week.

"Hey," I say attempting to cheer her up. "Do you still have the birthday party plans; they have to be amazing still!" We are planning a fun birthday sleepover for her birthday. So far I'm invited and I'm trying to get her to invite Rosie Dawkins.

"Yeah," She mumbles.

"Did your dad just call?" I ask, my voice turning serious.

"No, I was just thinking that my birthday's in three weeks." Caroline replies. I silently roll my eyes. Little Miss Worry is just about always thinking for the worst. Not that I don't feel bad, I do, but she always thinks about the bad things that could happen.

"Oh," I say. "Um, you know how I called and told you about how Rosie and I were planning a club?" She nods. "Well, I wanted to know if you wanted to join. It's going to be super fun, but a lot of work like fundraisers and things like that."

"What's it for?"

"Um, it sounds weird, but we wanted to name it – 'The Baseball Club for Girls', like a baseball club for us. We could play with the boys and show them whose boss. I came up with a motto and everything! 'We'll show you how to hit like a girl', cute huh?"

Caroline sinks into the seat in my bedroom and looks around. I've being dreaming of this since that day I wasn't allowed to play with the boys during practice. I'm a pretty big girly girl, but this one sport, I love and when I'm not even allowed to play it, that's a problem for me.

"So, what'd you think?" I wonder.

Caroline looks away and picks up the folder I made of things Rosie and I discussed and all of my mottos and fundraiser ideas. "I don't know," She finally spits out.

I look at my feet. I thought that Caroline of all people would love the idea since her dad won't be home for her birthday because he announces for baseball. I'm proven wrong.

"Um, okay." I say back, rolling my eyes to the back of my head. "I just thought it would be a good idea." Someone knocks on my door. Rosie enters my room showing a giant smile on her face.

"So, Baseball Club for Girls! What's up?" Alexandria Waters is behind her. We had a plan yesterday. She would talk to Alex about our idea and I would talk to Caroline. I'm suddenly wishing I'd gotten Alex.

I shake my head. "She said no."

"What!?" Rosie beams. "How could your grandma say no? It isn't even possible. She was so totally on board yesterday!" Rosie Dawkins can be so stupid sometimes.

"No, Rosie!" I say. "Caroline said no! She said she 'didn't know'." I feel bad calling Caroline out in front of Rosie and Alex and everything, but I have no choice. She should hear how ridiculous she sounds for herself.

"Listen, Caroline." Rosie sits on my bed going into a weird/angry mode. "I need this. I don't want to be just a cheerleader throughout middle school. I don't want to join chess club or anything either, I'm not that awful, but I do want to play a sport. Baseball is pretty much my only option."

I shake my head at the floor. Since when is Chess another option as a sport? Rosie can be so totally clueless sometimes.

Caroline doesn't look Rosie in the eye. She doesn't look anyone in the eye. "I guess it wouldn't be so bad," She says looking away.

"Yes!" Rosie cries. "Thanks! Okay, so it's settled. The baseball club for girls is finally here!" She leaps around my room and finally sighing and sliding into my small bean bag chair. "What should we do first?"

"Well," I say. "I guess cover the ground rules. I mean, what should be the, uh, ground rules?"

"Always be there for each other," Rosie suggests.

"Lame," Alex mumbles.

"Teamwork," Caroline squeaks.

"Isn't that pretty basic?" Alex murmurs.

"Honesty," Rosie declares.

"I'm honestly saying that's stupid," Alex snaps.

"Oh," I say. "What about you, Alex? What ideas for ground rules do you have?" I look her deep in her eyes and lock in on her so that she knows I'm not fooling around. I mean business.

"Fine," She says. She stands on her feet, well as much as a person on crutches can stand on two feet. "I think first off no quitting. I'm sorry, but when the going gets tough no one said to give up. No way, nuh-uh."

"Maybe," says Rosie. "But doesn't that kind of cover teamwork? Caroline said that and you said it was too basic." Alex doesn't stop to think for a second.

"Teamwork is basic, and it's totally different. Quitting is not only letting your team down, but yourself also. I don't think quitting solves anything in life." Alex replies.

"I think honesty is important." Caroline says sheepishly. "I'm just saying, I don't think people should say the wrong point as a lie so they win."

"Everything you just said," Alex sasses. "is so wrong! Okay, so say they are lying, you can't really prove anything and let me tell you, this game is skin and bones and if you aren't prepared to shed a tear you aren't prepared for this game."

I stand back stunned. Alex Waters is more effective than I thought. At first I thought she was just being a smart mouth and trying to get attention, but she's clearly right. This game is tough and girls like Caroline need to truly understand that or we will get our butts kicked.

"So," Alex continues. "That being said I'm pretty sure that you want me out." Rosie has this look on her face saying that she wants nothing more to do with Alex. I, on the other hand, think that her attitude might be perfect for baseball.

"No stay totally!" Rosie insists in a sarcastic tone. She points toward the door. "But, yeah you can find your way out."

I grab Rosie's arm and yank it hard. She squeals. "No stay seriously," I tell Alex. "We need you, but uh, Rosie if you want to find the door it's totally open for you!"

"Oh shut up," Rosie smiles. "Sorry, just don't be so bossy." She says to Alex.

"As long as you aren't," Alex shoots back, but in a friendly way smiling.

"It's settled," Caroline says. "The Baseball Club for Girls is official!" We all cheer and scream, only to find my two twin foster brothers, Jamal and Rak, come out from under my bed eavesdropping.

Alex

"Oh my gosh," I take off my shoe and massage my foot. Nobody knows how to dance apparently and so I'm the one who has to pay for this with a sore foot that's been stepped on probably half a million thousand times. I'm still upset that I can't even dance that well. My stupid ankle is preventing me from it. It's pretty much healed, but I still need to wear a wrap around it.

"I'm here!" shouts Gwen Biggley from the entrance dressed in her POM apparel. The practice for that is just a couple rooms down from the dance room. Because Gwen feels the need to have to be so amazing and popular she made her mom make her a resignation slip for quitting dance and there's one thing I hate more than anything in the world: quitting.

"Hello, Genevieve," Coach Linda says sharply with her lips pressed together. Coaches don't love quitting so much either, the one thing I'm happy about though, is that I will be seeing Gwen so much less often than every weekday after school.

Lauren Biggley, Gwen's mom, follows suit behind her with files of papers. Gwen's mom has always scared me, even when I was a kid and best friends with Gwen. She's super duper big. (Hint here, *Big*gley) Not like fat, but tall and a bit on the chunky side. She also is mean and because Gwen and I are no longer best friends forever like we were in second grade, she hates me.

"I have forms I need you to sign, Ms. Linda Keepshaw." Mrs. Biggley says handing her the stack of papers that looks as if it weighs in at ten pounds. "I need them back by the end of today."

"Mrs. Biggley," Coach Linda says handing the papers back. "I understand that Gwen is quitting, I don't need to go to court about it. No suing or harm done this is not a federal issue."

"I see your point," Mrs. Biggley insists. "Maybe you don't understand this through my eyes, though, Ms. Keepshaw. Say, there is a problem with her resignation, I need to have some signed documents testifying that Genevieve quit on this very day in September. Understood?"

"No," Coach Linda snaps. "I have a dance class to teach," She says. "I don't have any more time to sign papers for your daughters quitting. I don't approve of the quitting and I don't like the fact that you are making me do this and you can't."

"Excuse me, but -."

"NO!" Coach Linda shouts. "Now you are dismissed from my dance studio unless that is you are signing back up for this very dance class."

Stunned, Gwen and her mother reach for the door and exit. "Alright!" yells Coach Linda. "Enough chitchat you had more than enough rest, it's time to work!"

We start our first routine, which is basic. Without some of the girls here, it's harder to do, but we manage and when I have to be twirled around and flipped over its done so perfectly I am moved to the center of the group in front for the routine.

"Do you have to leave early today?" asks Coach Linda looking at the clock. I nod. Ever since the baseball club for girls started, dance has been a huge issue. I hate having to miss parts of the routines and not knowing what happened while I'm gone and of course missing the fights that Linda has with moms and dads like the one with Gwen's mom.

"See ya then," I leave to look for the Taylor's minivan. Caroline's mom has had to drive me around because my parents don't 'prefer the idea' as they said. I go anyway because Mrs. Taylor assured me that I'd be great at it. She's my math teacher so she was especially happy to take me.

We've only had one 'meeting' and that was a parent meeting. I had to miss a tiny bit of dance and my parents, of course, didn't show. I was stuck sitting alone with all of the other girls and their parents.

Ruth Keener, our coach, and Jim Keener, our assistant coach, have done a good job explaining our goals as a team this year and next. I can't wait to start although I have to be on a team with Caroline Taylor, Rosie Dawkins, and Jackie Heaters. I mean, they're okay, but from what I've seen they don't look like they know much about baseball.

Ruth played in the 1940's when men were at World War II and there weren't many men to play baseball and her husband, Jim, played on the Boston Red Sox for ten years.

"Hi, sweetie." Mrs. Taylor greets me when I hop into the van. Her daughter Cece gives her an angry look.

"Mom, I was in the middle of a story." She snaps.

"I know, Cece, but Alex just got in the car and I thought we should greet her. Besides, you've told me how you got on the honor roll before the second semester about three times a day since Monday." Mrs. Taylor replies. "Hey, Caroline, say hi to your friend."

Caroline doesn't make a peep, but her little brother Cody and little sister Ashley beam when I sit in between them. "Hi!" jumps Cody.

"Hi Ally!" smiles Ashley.

I smile, if only everyone was as friendly as the Taylors. "Oh, hi Alex I didn't notice you. Sorry about that!" says Cece after she's done having a conversation with her mom.

"Oh hey," Caroline whispers to me. I ignore her. Caroline Taylor is the shyest and weirdest person ever. Why she wanted to join this club is a mystery to me. She and Jackie are friends, but since when do you do everything that your friends do? Besides, there's no crying in baseball and I will bet anything that with her around, there will be.

"Okay girls, I'll be right here at six okay? Caroline tell Miss Ruth if you need anything, k?" The car drops us off at 'The Michigan Athletic Center, where a lot of teams practice for sports and sometimes dance teams will use the studio. I've been only been in here one of two times and that was to watch a competition.

"Hello Caroline and Alexandria," Ruth says. I wave as she directs us towards the changing rooms. "You already look dressed in exercise wear."

"I came from dance," I explain and let Caroline meet Rosie and Jackie in the bathrooms. However, I decide to explore and check out the place where we will meet a lot. Ruth told us how we will have to be spending most time from September to December doing fundraisers for next summer when we start really playing baseball.

"I have organized a few fundraisers that will be occurring to raise money for the organization," Ruth said a few days ago at the parent meeting. "The girls, if choosing to join will have to devote some time into these extra activities."

We have to have bake sales and car washes and snow shoveling to raise money. The sad thing about that meeting was that only Jackie, Rosie, Caroline, and I showed up for it. There were flyers send out, but nobody seemed to like the idea. I guess it's going to take more than just one tiny flyer to get more people interested in the club.

"Okay girls!" Jim shouts when Jackie, Caroline, and Rosie return. "Who knows all of the positions?" My hand shoots up, but Jackie's only goes up halfway and Rosie and Caroline look lost. "Um, yes, Alex?"

"First, Second, Shortstop, and Third are in the infield and Right, Center, and Left are in the outfield. Plus the catcher and of course, the pitcher." I say proudly.

"I thought we had a fourth base." Rosie says confused.

"That's home plate," Jim says.

"Oh, isn't that a position with the mask and stuff? Oh and a glove?" Rosie continues.

"That's a catcher, Rosie." Jim replies. Rosie nods and smiles, looking away.

"I want to throw the ball at the batters," Rosie declares. "What is that again?"

"A pitcher," Jim answers her. "You can try that if you want." Rosie looks satisfied and it gets us through the rest of the questions. Even though I answered correctly, Jim makes us play a little trivia game remembering them all. Rosie gets none right because she believes in fourth base and Jackie only misses Pitcher, which she just forgot to include. Caroline gets them all right which surprises us. If Caroline really new all of this stuff why wouldn't she just speak up?

"Good job girls," Ruth says after the rest of practice. We hardly do anything. We finish up trivia when Rosie finally understands that there is no fourth base and then we do some warm-ups. It's boring and a waste of my time as far as I'm concerned. Rosie Dawkins knows nothing about baseball. I have no idea why she would ever want to learn. She's impossible.

Catching a ride from Mrs. Taylor, I hurry in the house. My mom is sipping her evening coffee and has the table set as my dad finishes reading the news. Nobody says hi, nobody says love you, nobody says anything. The room falls silent, like always.

I set my things down and try to be more noticeable. Nothing works. My parents are so into their articles and cooking that they don't even notice me. I even drop my crutches in attempt to see them boss me to pick them up, but they don't.

"Oh Alexandria," Mom says at dinner. "You were very late home from dance," My mom always talks super duper official like this because she talks with adults all day and feels the need to try and explain things thoroughly. "I suppose you recognized us not making an acquaintance when you proposed your arrival."

"I'm sorry," I groan. My parents feel the need to do this all the time. If only they 'preferred the idea' of two things at once, but no, that's too unorganized. They hate the whole thing. Baseball and they don't like that I'd be 'juggling' two things at once.

***

"So how long have you been in dance?" wonders Rosie. The breezy fall winds rush through my hair sweeping it into my face as I answer. Walking home isn't fun, even when the high is supposed to be at least sixty on a cold September day and you have a sprained ankle, no more crutches finally at least.

"That depends," I reply. "I did the basic four year old ballet when I was four, but I've done tap, hip hop, and now I'm in just the basics that they have at the community center."

Rosie's really nice and not as stupid as I thought she was. I thought she was going to be really dimwitted and one of those girls who pretends that they are so clueless about everything happening around them, but she's not. She's super nice, though.

"Tell me more about Adelynn Simone," I say. Her mom sounds like a pain to have to deal with. Always having to deal with a superstar doesn't sound like fun, but compared to what my mom does, it might be better.

"What's to tell?" She laughs. "I haven't seen her in like eight years and I'm actually supposed to move in a couple of months. Oh, but if you see Ruth don't tell her that I'm going to Paris. I don't want her to think that I'm quitting."

"Well are you?" I start to fidget. I hate quitters.

"I don't want to," Rosie sighs. "But in a nutshell, moving is mandatory if I ever want to help out my family."

"What's wrong with your family?" I wonder.

"Oh the obvious." I give her a confused look. "A couple of years back my grandparents reopened a tea shop to make money, but the business has been drastically coming to a fail and they need some real help so the plan is to help them."

I take a breath. "Wow," I say. "It almost sounds like a movie plot."

"That's a way to put it." She nods. "Anyway, we've been supposed to move forever and now it seems more realistic."

"Cool," I smile. "How long do you think this whole baseball thing will last?"

"Why do you mean?"

"I mean like, how impossible this is. We have four girls and no time."

"Well," She sighs. "I guess that's it then, it was just an idea of Jackie's. I don't think it will ever come through. I've learned that Jackie is sort of a dreamer."

"So am I," I mumble. "Only sometimes I wish dreams came true."

"They can," Rosie says. "But most of the time they don't so, yeah."

"Whatever," I say. I just want the baseball club for girls to make a difference.

Rosie

"One-thousand words?" I hand my paper back to my teacher. "I thought it was a hundred." This day has been fun. Ms. Jones refuses to grade my paper unless I rewrite it with more words. That will take forever and I don't have that much time on my hands.

"Rosie just do it, I'm giving you until Monday." The good thing, I won't be here Monday. My dad finally saved enough money to at least get us on the plane so in a few days I'll be in Paris with my mom and I'll be famous possibly, it all just kind of depends on the mark I leave as Adelynn Simone's daughter.

My dad and I are all packed now and a week from now will be my last day of school. I am so excited, only kind of disappointed. My new baseball friends are nice now. A great thing about them is that they're good to talk to, but I don't have to be their best friend.

"R-R-Rosie!" Gwen Biggley shouts. I turn around and smile. Since being on the Pon Pom squad Gwen had been so nice. I know that Alex has strictly warned me to avoid any friendships with her, but you know, Alex can be bossy.

"Hey, Hey," I say and give her a hug. "So, I was thinking that for the dance we need to perform 'Scares and Dreaming'." Gwen nods. Every year the school has a Halloween dance and every year the Pon Pom squad performs. This year we have to.

"We aren't performing that," says Sydney Mister, another girl on the team. "I just heard that the principal told Alex Waters that it was her job to write the song."

"Are you kidding?" Gwen freaks. I feel guilty suddenly. It's not my fault that she hates Alex, but I do hang out with Gwen a lot now and it makes me feel bad that I just allow myself to listen to Gwen bully Alex.

Although Alex is doing much better hobbling around now without crutches on her broken ankle, she still can't dance or play that well. She's been writing songs a lot, so it's not surprise they picked her, well and her dad kind of owns this district and the school so that might play it's part in it, but still. It's not like I'm super popular because of my mom's stardom. To tell the truth, not many people know who my mom is, but she's an actress in Paris so many French people know her.

Gwen flips her hair around and stares at the ground. "This is so unfair."

Sydney nods and I suddenly feel like I should too, but I don't. I'm not that kind of person. I hang out with Gwen and I hang out with Alex, but no way will I ever let them make fun of each other with me around. I don't, and probably never will put up with that.

"I wish that Alex Waters would just go away somehow," Sydney comments.

"That would be amazing," Gwen sighs.

I think about walking away, after all I'm not sure if Sydney and Gwen are real friend material and anyway, I don't need to know people who just gossip about everyone and anyone they can think of.

"Hey Rose," Jackie passes me in the hallway. I smile regretting what I said to Alex about her yesterday. Jackie is a big dreamer, but when I told Alex that I said it like it was a bad thing and it isn't.

I'm becoming better friends with Jackie and Alex, but I'm not so sure where Caroline is. It almost seems as if she just doesn't want to do anything with us or practice and throws Ally under the bus because of her leg.

That's the thing with Jackie, Alex, and I. We can call each other a million other nicknames. Alex I sometimes say 'Dria' or 'Ally' and we call Jackie 'Maggs' because of her mom and because of the Detroit Tigers.

They call me Rosie, Rose, Ro-Ro. The name count is endless. To me, however, Caroline is just Caroline and will never be anything else, unless she changes her name or something.

"Hey Maggs," I say back and she sticks her tongue out at me. Gwen and Sydney do a double-take at this.

"Um, sorry Rosie, but we don't hang with her or any of them." Sydney explains. I knew there was a catch to hanging out with the more popular girls. Sydney nervously looks over at Gwen, who is biting her lip cautiously.

"Well, why not?" I ask.

Sydney sighs. Gwen, who seems frazzled and freaked out, stands in front of the lockers and gives me a sad look telling me to stop now. The thing is, I'm not sure what I'm doing.

"You see," Sydney explains. "Alex and Jackie and you know, Caroline they aren't, how do I put this?"

"Cool enough for you?" I wonder.

"Us," Sydney says. "Us, we are all friends here, come on Ro, I thought Gwen, you, and I were the besties. Look, your other 'acquaintances' are okay we suppose, but just think about what they'll bring you."

"I don't think anything," I reply confused.

"Exactly," Sydney says. "Don't you understand now? They will bring you nothing. That is why you're so much better off with us." Sydney flips back her hair and smiles. "It's better this way."

I give a worried glance towards Alex and Jackie who are laughing and Caroline who walks up to them with cookies and mugs of hot chocolate. I can't possibly let Caroline Taylor take my place as Jackie and Alex's friend. Sure, Caroline is in the Baseball Club for Girls, but still.

"Rosie," snaps Gwen, taking me out of my daydream. "Why aren't you coming, I've been saying your name like a million times."

"Oh," I say. I stare at the floor as I walk away from my friends, well my old friends. "Where are you going?"

"Outside, duh," Sydney replies. Gwen gives me a sharp look.

"Um, I don't really want to go outside, it's cold out and um, I didn't bring a jacket with me today."

"We're going outside." Gwen says. "Come or stay your choice, I don't care. I know you'd rather stay with Jackie and them." Gwen's sad face drags me closer to her and Sydney.

"No never mind," I smile. "I want to hang out with you guys. We should practice that routine that we just learned."

"I was thinking more of shopping at the mall." Gwen suggests.

"Oh, yeah!" Sydney nods.

"That works," I manage to mumble.

***

"Hold my bags," Gwen demands as we work our way back to the main entrance of the middle school building where Mrs. Biggley promised to meet us when our shopping was over. I can't believe I had to walk to the mall and then hold Gwen's bags the entire way back.

"OMG, Gwen that was so fun!" Sydney cries. I swear everything that she says is just fake and to get attention. She says nothing interesting, but the shopping trip was fun and I got some sportswear for practice.

Gwen strolls on down to the bleachers to sit down and watch the boys practice. "I want my coat." She says and Sydney grabs it out of one of the bags. Happily, Gwen puts it on and smiles. "You guys are so amazing," She says to Jackson Spicer.

"Thanks," Jackson replies.

"Oh no problem, I wish that I could play." Gwen bats her eyes and silently demands for lip gloss from Sydney who hands it over.

"You can," Jackson says. "Out coach is allowing that today. Sydney and Rosie, right? You guys can play too."

Gwen's face goes blank. "Um, nah, I don't know." Sydney nods at this and I nod too. I've started to learn to just agree with Gwen, it then makes life a lot earlier.

"No you should," Jackson coaxes.

My face brightens up. I need help and practice and maybe I can get Gwen and Sydney to join our club too! Fat chance, though.

"No thanks," Gwen denies the offer. "Come on girls, I think the gym is open for us to dance."

I go as followed. Might as well dance until Gwen's mom takes me home.

The only sad thing, I bet if I were with Caroline, Alex, and Jackie they might want to play, but too late now I'm friends with the amazing, popular, Gwen Biggley.

I'm not sure whether to like that or not.

Caroline

"Okay," I reply into the phone, my voice shaky and uncertain as I hand the phone to my sister who takes it with her hand unsteady. Cece grabs the hand and looks from Cody, to Ashley, to me wondering if she should talk into it. I nod in a silent reply.

"Um, hey," she says, sounding more like the preppy Cece, only she isn't right now. Dad just called and he pretty much just upset me again saying he didn't know about my birthday, but he had a pretty great gift. All I want for my birthday is him to be home with me, not in stupid Washington to announce a sports game.

Mom walks into the room. She hasn't been too happy either, but she knows that I need the most help, since in two weeks it's my birthday. She says that even though his job makes him a jerk and this isn't fair, he has a great present. I know he's not coming back in time.

"Bye Dad," Cece hangs the phone up and the room falls silent. Nobody has anything to say. Ashley and Cody know what's wrong too and they want me to have Daddy on my birthday. Sometimes I feel selfish, but then I don't because he should be here on my birthday.

"It was nice of Daddy to call, right guys?" Cece asks to Ashley and Cody to make us them feel less awkward. They nod and Mom shoots Cece a sympathy look. "You know what he'd really like," Cece says to them. "Cards from you guys, he'd love that. You can use my sparkly glitter, Ash, and Cody I think I have some stickers you can use."

"Thanks Cece," Mom smiles. My sister really can be super nice sometimes.

"Caroline, do you want to make a card too?" Cece asks. Then sometimes she can be a real pain, like now.

I shake my head in anger that she would ask something so stupid. He should be making me a card, not me making him one! Easy for Cece to blow this whole thing off, she wouldn't care if he was gone on her birthday. She can and will get over anything, she never, ever holds grudges.

"Caroline," Mom says patting the seat next to her; I move sitting next to her. "I'm sorry that Daddy isn't here and that he won't be here for your birthday,"

I nod to her, but in my head I'm furious. If people are so sorry, why do they keep bringing it up? I just want to skip my birthday this year so that I won't have to keep being reminded about how much I want him to be here.

"Sweetie, Daddy sent your present now because he thought it was a good birthday party idea for you." She hands me a package with cards inside of it, but now just any cards. There are five tickets to the Tigers V.S. Mariners game on October 15th, my birthday!

"Oh my gosh," I glow up like a Christmas tree. "Really, who do I bring?"

"Well, one of these tickets is for me and one is for you and the rest are for whoever you choose." I think for a second. Jackie, Alex, Rosie and I were planning a super duper sleepover with my sister making everything for it, but this just sounds like more fun.

"Jackie, Rosie, and Alex I guess." I jump off my seat and smile. I'm so excited, maybe there's hope in seeing my dad on my birthday after all, but then there's a note in the package.

Hey Princess,

I'm so sorry, but while the game is in Michigan, I have to host sports awards that same day. I wish I could be there, I really do and I wish you the very best birthday wishes.
Love,
Daddy

I let a tear drop on the package. This isn't fair again. I don't want this to happen. It's almost as if he's avoiding my birthday all together and making up for it with this? I just don't understand.

"Caroline!" Mom calls. "We're going now!" I grab my jacket and run downstairs in a hurry to beat Ashley and Cody who are racing each other. Now we tumble and Cody sprawls out on the floor pretending he's dead.

"Don't act like that in the store," demands Cece. We nod. I might be the second oldest, but I can have my fun too and Cece can't stop that.

Cece has a part-time job at Midnight Sweets down the street from our house. I sometimes help her, but that's because our Aunt Reba and Uncle Rob own the place so we get jobs without applications. It sounds like a normal bakery, but it's not. They make the kookiest cakes and baked goods that no normal bakery can make and my sister has had her chance to do so too.

For the first day of school Mom asked Aunt Reba to make a cake to give us some luck. Mostly just Cece and I as we entered either Middle School or High School. Aunt Reba was going to make her signature fall cake, but instead she made the 'school girls (and boys, for Cody) cake' in which was a big school made of cupcakes on top with strawberry frosting. The regular cream cheese frosting was on top along with cookies and cream cake batter inside. It sounds kind of gross, but it was the best cake ever.

Cece says that she, Uncle Rob, and Aunt Reba have something cooking up for my birthday and because the bakery has food as well, we're making mini pizzas and cupcakes tonight. Aunt Reba and Uncle Rob have a room in the back where they eat their dinner every night and said that we could use it tonight.

"Hello!" Aunt Reba yells giving us all big hugs. "Come on in! Cece your Uncle Rob has a cake all ready for you to make." Cece puts on her smock on and walks back while we examine all of the cakes on display. We ooh and ahh at all of the 'super duper fall creations'.

"We have so many things right now that we're making at once. We have a princess birthday cake in the back, miss Ashley, I know that your Uncle Rob could use some extra help." Ashley runs to the back to help.

"Cody, we have a robot cake too, one of our workers could use some help!" Cody races back. I admire all of the cakes, especially one with peanut butter frosting.

"Ah, you know Cece said you liked peanut butter," Aunt Reba says.

"I love peanut butter anything," I say smiling.

"Well, then you're in store today. We have a couple coming in who wants a peanut butter wedding cake. I could really use some help." I can't even think about it before I say yes. How can my Aunt Reba have such a cool job and Dad have such a stupid one?

A few people walk in and Aunt Reba goes into full on 'I love my job' mode. "Hello! Welcome to Midnight Sweets, my name is Reba Boomer, what can I get you on this fine evening?"

This is a bakery and a diner, my uncle Rob handles all the orders in his diner. She talks like that at the front desk.

"Um, I'll take a fresh loaf of bread and a dozen birthday cake cupcakes." The lady says. Birthday Cake Cupcakes are legendary. They are frozen ice cream cupcakes with cake batter inside and whipped cream frosting. The best ever!

"Can I interest you in a free sample of our new limited-time-only special banana split cupcake?" Aunt Reba asks in her southern accent.

"Ew, no thanks," The lady shakes her head.

"They're delicious," I speak up in my shy voice.

"I'll try it," She says. Once shoved into her mouth she asks for a dozen of those too. I stare amazed that Aunt Reba just got the costumer to buy more than she wanted by a free sample.

"Also," my aunt goes and grabs a coffee pot marked 'Midnight Truffle Mocha – Rob's'. "Saying thanks for buying our signature birthday cake cupcakes, a loaf of fresh bread, and banana split cupcakes we offer you a cup of coffee for free."

"I would say no, but I kind of want some coffee to go with all of this. What sizes do you have?"

"We give out smalls for free, but with an additional twenty cents I can get you a medium,"

"I'll take a medium," the costumer says grabbing twenty cents out of her purse. I smile at Aunt Reba, amazed. This is crazy.

"Thank you for your purchase, your total is twenty-eighty-nine." The costumer walks out with her cupcakes, coffee, and bread. Mom and I stare at Aunt Reba.

"Reba, isn't that a low cost for so many items?" Mom asks.

"Maybe," Reba answers. "But the good thing is that we will have a returning costumer, which makes more money a lot, not just in one sale. Please, let me do my job. Now y'all think you're ready to run the front counter?"

"I think so," Mom replies. "As long as you wrote me a script because there is no way I can possibly say everything you just did." Aunt Reba hands her a piece of paper as I wander off to the back of the shop where Cody and the workers are making a vanilla robot cake and Ashley and Uncle Rob are making a strawberry shortcake princess birthday party cake. Cece is busy alone putting the finishing touches on a display cake she made.

"Isn't Aunt Reba amazing at the front counter?" Cece asks. "I could never do that. Here, help with this frosting disaster that ruined my cake." I grab the tools out of her hand and attempt to fix the small spill on the countertop.

"This place is so cool," I say looking around at the creations in the windows. "What's the peanut butter surprise?" I ask. "My birthday cake I presume."

"Nope, sorry sis," Cece replies. "I'm not going to say a word about your cake."

I sigh. I really want to know what Aunt Reba, Uncle Rob, and Cece are doing to my cake. I can already taste Aunt Reba's amazing peanut butter frosting that she makes, but I want to know what the rest is made of.

Sometimes I wish that I lived with Uncle Rob and Aunt Reba, they're always have fun. Mom right now is really stressed out about her job. She's only a math teacher at my school, but I can tell she just wishes Dad would quit his job. Most families cringe when someone looses their job, but Mom would be more than happy right now.

Cece returns from the very back fridge with frosting all over her face and hair and smock. I start to laugh just before she swats me with a dirty rag and I grab the frosting tub and pour it over her.

"Caroline!" She shrieks. "I know you want a hug," She tries to come and hug me, but I sneak a cake off the table and throw it in her face. "Oh my gosh!" She screams.

"What?"

"That cake is supposed to be picked up today and now it's in on my face!" Cece yells.

"Uh-oh," I say.

"That's all you can say?" She screams. "Uh-oh? We've got to do something! They probably need that and now we ruined it! I spent a lot of time on that and now, now it's ruined!"

"Hey gals," trots in Aunt Reba. "What happened?" She stops in her tracks. "I know y'all want to say that this isn't the wedding cake because if it is that couple is here now and it's been late already."

"Uh, we were having a little fun in the kitchen and uh, Caroline didn't realize that she grabbed their lovely wedding cake and um, it's all over me now." Cece explains. I nod.

"Well, I'm not so thrilled about this, but because I know you want to repay me, go and talk it up with those two, while I try and substitute and cake and attempt to clean up this disaster."

Cece and I make a turn for the front counter and put on hammy smiles to the couple who already look irritated.

"You are?" Cece asks.

"Missy Wilder," The lady says.

"Johnny Young," The man answers.

"Uh, so you guys are getting married?" Cece asks she swats me to start talking to them, but I'm so shy I just stand beside my sister. I'm way too shy to say anything to strangers.

"Yup," Johnny answers. "Our friends said that the best cakes in town were from here and I thought we'd try a cake and then when we liked it we decided that our wedding cake had to be kooky and fun, like us."

Cece awes at this and shows them the cake catalog and even offers them some cupcakes and muffins because of their cake being so late.

"When are you getting married?" I ask.

74

"Tomorrow," Missy snaps. "We're late to our own rehearsal dinner! We were going to take the cake now so that way we'd make this easier on ourselves, but since it isn't ready. We could just order from Quick Cakes, Johnny."

"No!" cries Cece. "Your cake will be ready soon, I promise. You can't order from Quick Cakes, they don't even use really frosting they use boxed frosting because they're cheap and quick! Trust me, one year my mom forgot to order me a cake for my party so we had to buy one from that place. Yuck, worst ever."

I stare at the floor. Quick Cakes actually has some decent cakes and I know that the only reason Cece is doing this is to save Aunt Reba and make conversation. I'm sorry that we ruined their wedding cake and I know that Aunt Reba will make us pay for this, but right now we just need to make them happy.

"We need to go now," Johnny says.

"Hello everyone," Uncle Rob says pouring himself some coffee. "Do you have your cake? I can go look for it. Is there a problem?"

"No problem!" insists Cece.

"Um, we're getting married tomorrow and would like it if we had our cake." Missy says.

"Where is it?"

"That's what we'd like to know," Johnny shoots back. Cece and I look at each other. This is about to get bad with Uncle Rob here. I wish we hadn't had our cake fight. Then we wouldn't be in this mess.

"Young, right?" Uncle Rob checks the last name. He touches the order screen. "Your cake was ready about an hour ago."

"Thank you!" Missy sighs. "Can we have it? We have a rehearsal to get to!"

"It's not in the back, though." I say.

"Well, girls, where is it?" Uncle Rob asks.

"You're looking at it," Cece says pointing to herself and letting them examine the cake pieces on her.

"SOMEBODY BETTER FIX THIS, NOW!" Missy screams. "I HAVE A WEDDING TO GET TO AND I WANT MY CAKE! NOW! I'M GOING TO WRITE YOU UP! JOHNNY, ORDER A QUICK CAKE NOW!"

"I heard yelling," Aunt Reba returns with a perfectly new cake. "Was there some sort of problem?"

"My cake, where is my wedding cake?" Missy beams. "I'm getting married in a day and I need my cake."

"Right here, peanut butter frosting and cookies and cream cake," Johnny smiles at Missy and she gives him a sad look. I can only imagine if my I heard somebody ruined my wedding cake.

"Thank you," Johnny says and him and Missy leave admiring the cake and hurrying up to get to their rehearsal.

"How'd you bake that in the last fifteen minutes?" Cece wonders. Aunt Reba forces a giant smile.

"I took one of these extra cakes from the back and re-frosted it to say the wedding information they requested." Aunt Reba explains. Cece and I stare at our aunt, openmouthed and astonished that she made a wedding cake that fast and it still looked great.

"Wow," Cece says.

"I know you girls are going to clean up that mess of a kitchen back there and going to write a nice apology note to those two for delaying their wedding cake."

Cece and I look at each other and nod. We head to the back kitchen to notice that Aunt Reba didn't think of us one bit when she was frosting her cake because there is frosting all over the walls and a mess of cake on the tables.

"Well," I take another look around. "That's what we get." We grab rags and start to wipe clean off the counters and tables.

Jackie

Murray takes a moment to look in the mirror again and readjust the table again. I have no idea why my dad visiting is such a big deal to her. Jamal and Rak and the other kids are going crazy too. Maybe it's because they don't have my dad – a dad I mean. They don't have any parents.

My dad is flying in from San Diego. It's the first time he's been home since he moved to San Diego a couple of months ago. Sometimes thinking about only living with my grandparents and foster kids makes me feel like I'm up for adoption like the kids here.

"Behave yourselves," Grandma demands to Rak and Jamal who are picking at each other's ears. I shoot them a disgusted look and they stop, even they want to meet my father.

"Okay, I've got the whole agenda for this weekend," Murray says pulling out a white board and showing it to everyone. "First things first Mr. Heaters will be tired from his long flight and time change and probably want some space so, kids, I know that I said card exchange was first, but I need that to come tomorrow."

I stare at her confused. What about my dad visiting with me and my grandparents? Did she ever think of that when she made her agenda?

"Then, later tonight I have a special dinner planned for our guest and a dessert, that is, if you guys are on your best behavior." Murray continues. "Tomorrow is the tour of the home and a trip to Home Town for Jamal, Rak, Suzy, Marie, Bailey, Jon, and Junior."

I roll my eyes. Murray can't plan my dad for me besides I'm going to Caroline's birthday party tomorrow. Murray even arranged for a little field trip to take the smaller kids on so that they can stay out of trouble while my dad stays.

"Sunday, I have a lunch at Julio's planned for Ms. Ruth, Mr. Jim, Mr. Heaters, Junior and I." Murray goes on. My jaw drops. I don't even get to have lunch with my dad, but Murray and Junior get to? How could my grandparents ever let her schedule this!?

"When do we get to meet Jackie's dad?" shouts Suzy.

"You need to be sure to address him as Mr. Heaters, Suzy." Murray corrects her. "I'm not certain on that. This weekend will be the fun and it's up to him what he's doing next week."

My face turns hot. The kids, who are dying to meet him, don't even get to all because Murray didn't schedule it?! I don't understand why my dad needs to be on a schedule and why I'm not on it!

"Anyway, to know exactly what you're doing I have schedules over here and a list of things for everyone to know about our special guest." Murray finishes.

Grandma squeezes my shoulders when I start to tense up in my shoulders because I'm so angry. "Wasn't it nice of Murray to make this up for Daddy?"

"When do I get to spend time with him?" I wonder. "Why do only she, Junior and all of you get to go out to lunch with him?" Grandma presses her lips together and sighs. I'm being difficult, but he is my dad, not Murray's.

"If you really want to come to Julio's, I suppose it would be fine, but Murray and Junior have some business that they want to discuss with Daddy some work to do. Murray needs to have him be her d-,." Grandma explains. I can hardly imagine the things

Murray has already cooked up. I don't allow her to finish, I go to the door to wait for my dad.

The doorbell rings and the kids rush to the couch and sit in a line. They smiles on their faces and look as excited as can be.

The reason they don't know my dad is because my mom, my dad, and I lived in a house down the street before Mom died and Dad moved for his job. When Dad moved, Grandma moved me too – into the foster home with the kids.

Murray and Junior rush to the door first. My dad walks in with a suitcase behind him and he smiles at me. I go to hug him when Murray steps on my foot in front of me. "Hello, so glad to meet you, Mr. Heaters my name is Murray Lockwood. Did you get my email?"

"What email?" I snap.

Just when I think for a second Murray might be in my way this week, my dad steps away from her and ignores her. He throws his arms around me and smiles. "I missed you, sweetie."

Murray looks a little appalled. She puts her hands on her hips and starts whispering something to

Junior. He nods. I don't even care for a second, I'm just happy to see my dad.

"Um, uh, hello, Mr. Heaters," She steps back in and gives him a card. "I planned a marvelous dinner tonight and some time for you to relax, but we wanted to introduce ourselves. Again, I'm Murray just wondering about that email -,"

"Hold on, Miss Lockwood, but I'm not sure that I need all that tonight. I was hoping to spend time with my daughter." My dad says. Junior shoots Murray a nervous look. She ignores him and hands my dad a schedule.

"I've prepared the weekend," She announces. "The rest of the week is yours to choose. We're taking the kids – Junior's taking the kids – to the Home Town Carnival tomorrow. I am going to stay back and tidy the house."

"Hey, Jackie do you want to go to that Home Town Carnival thing?" Junior says as if on cue. "I got an extra ticket." Murray smiles and nods at Junior as if what he said was an award winning speech. She planned this to get rid of me, but it's not going to work.

"No thank you," I reply. Murray and Junior exchange another glance, this time it screams angry

83

and they both look away quickly. "Daddy, what do you want to do tomorrow?"

"I'd like to visit the stadium. I heard they're taking pictures before tomorrow's game!" I smile. I can't wait to actually go to that game! Caroline's birthday party is at the game and I'm so excited.

"Uh, Mr. Heaters." Murray jumps back into the conversation. "We have a strict, very hard worked on schedule to follow so I think it would be best to stay task. Tomorrow I have an amazing day planned for you."

"Does it include going to the stadium?"

"No," She snaps. "Maybe you should find your own time, the rest of the week, to visit because I'd like us all to stick together."

"This is his vacation," I start to get snippy. "He should do what he wants and maybe he doesn't want where you want to go. How can you even possibly know what to do with him? He's not your father!"

"Jackie, please." Dad insists.

"Maybe I need him more than you!" Murray screams. She hurries into her bedroom and starts to cry. Grandma chases after her and so does Grandpa,

84

but Dad stays put. He sits down on the couch and sighs at me.

"Jackie, I know you're upset that she is trying to take over my weekend and be my daughter, but you have to be nice. She just wants parents, not like Grandparents like Ruth and Jim, but real ones."

"How do you know?" I ask puzzled. It seems like he knows Murray better than I do.

"Don't all foster children? She wants a dad for the weekend, Jackie." He says.

"I do too!" I exclaim. "I barely see you at all, doesn't she know that? I want you to me this week. Not having her with you the whole time!"

Dad pats my back. He understands, maybe Murray and Junior just don't. They don't understand that he's my dad first, not theirs.

Dinner is arranged to be Dad's favorite for his first day back and he adores all of the kids and has a great night watching his favorite movie with us all. It's a really fun night and I'm glad he's home.

Alex

I plead once more, begging to get out of the house and go to a birthday party. The party starts any minute now, but because my parents are so strict about where the party is at, and why, and when is it happening, and who is invited, they won't let me go to Caroline Taylor's birthday party, I don't have any high hopes for a Caroline Taylor birthday party, but she may surprise us with the party agenda.

"Do you know what you're doing at the party?" Mom asks in her stern, 'I'm in an authority position', voice. I make a face, but only to the side. To be honest, I have no idea, I just know I'm invited and so are Rosie and Jackie.

There's a knock on the door before I can answer her question. My dad goes to answer it and Caroline's family's minivan is in the driveway. Cece, Caroline's sister, is at the door.

"Hello, Mr. and Mrs. Waters, I'm here for Alex." Cece says. My mom smirks at my dad and I can tell that both of them are about to go into 'drill mode' which means they are about to annoy Cece with questions.

"Alexandria isn't allowed out until I know exactly what is happening at this party," my dad says.

"Uh, okay, it's a sleepover and I made a cake and well, that's about it. We're going out to dinner -,"

"Where to?" My mom asks.

"We're not sure yet, Caroline hasn't decided. Either Pizza Township, Eat it or Beat it, or Burger Ports." Cece answers. My parents hate Eat it or Beat it and Burger Ports. Pizza Township is 'okay' to them, but they prefer rich places like Julio's. My parents only like food that is worth eating. That's how they put it.

"Okay," My dad says and my mom nods. "Be good," They demand to me. I nod my head and leave with Cece. Jackie and Caroline are in the car already.

"I thought you'd never come out!" Mrs. Taylor says when we get in the car. "I'm starving!"

"Pizza Township," Caroline shouts to her mother. "Its right by here that way we can eat quicker." Everyone sighs happily. I haven't been to Pizza

Township since my eighth birthday party and we had the best pizza ever there.

"Now," Cece says turning back to Jackie, Caroline, and I. "I have tonight's super fun party agenda for you!"

"Sounds like Murray," Jackie whispers to us, we start to giggle.

"First, dinner at Pizza Township, second I present to you a night of baseball!" She gives us tickets to tonight's baseball playoff came at the stadium. I look at Caroline with my mouth open.

"How'd you get these?" I wonder.

"My dad sent them," She replies in a whisper.

"So he's in town now for your birthday, right?" Jackie wonders.

"No," Caroline mumbles. "He's in another state to do a baseball special this week." Jackie looks at the ground. I would feel bad too if I had asked that question.

"After the game, we're going to Midnight Sweets to have a special birthday cake that my aunt Reba and I made!" Cece continues.

"Won't it be like midnight when we get to the shop?" Caroline asks her sister.

"Yeah," replies Cece. "But its Midnight at Midnight Sweets, isn't that the point?"

We park in the driveway at Pizza Township and the service is instant. They sit us down and bring out cheesy bread and sauce as soon as we set our things down. I dig in, I'm starving, and so does everyone else.

"What can I get everyone?" The waitress asks us.

"I'll have some water and 'the best pizza ever'," Mrs. Taylor reads from the menu.

"I want the 'surprise me, surprise pizza," Cece says.

"Birthday sauce?" curiously asks Caroline.

"Oh, it has sprinkles and well, basically it's just frosting." The waitress replies.

"Can I have that?" asks Caroline. Mrs. Taylor nods and so does the waitress.

"I want the cheese pizza," says Jackie.

"I'll have pepperoni pizza," I order. I feel so plain with everyone picking special pizzas, but I'm not choosing a random food from the menu, and I'm not the birthday girl. I look around the restaurant for a second before I realize something's missing. "Is Rosie here?" I ask.

"No," Caroline whispers under her breath. "She stood me up for Gwen Biggley's spa day party." I look away and roll my eyes. I warned Rosie about her long before Caroline even said anything about a party and Rosie didn't listen to me. What can I say, I tried?

"Her loss," Jackie says. I nod. Rosie says that her dad finally bought plane tickets and that they're leaving in a week.

Our food comes and we eat it up quickly. I didn't realize how good Pizza Township was, my mom makes soups a lot and other than that my dad takes us out to a fancy place and Pizza Township is not a fancy place.

On our way to the game the clouds start to cast over us, worrying Mrs. Taylor. Of course this freaks out Caroline, who thinks this the worst thing that could ever happen, but I assure her that there is no way that a few storm clouds are going to rain on her birthday.

But I stand corrected by the weather.

We arrive at the stadium when it starts to sprinkle. Little drops and I guess that Mrs. Taylor forgot they rain ponchos. "I didn't think it was supposed to rain,"

By the time the game starts – it stops. Cece takes over Rosie's ticket because she isn't here and is stressing out because she has expensive shoes on and they're ruined.

"What are those people doing?" I ask my friends and Cece and Mrs. Taylor when I see people moving.

"Going home,"

"Why?" I wonder.

"It's raining," says Cece.

"Weren't these tickets expensive and what if the sky clears up, they might have wasted their money on a good game."

"I'm about to leave," Cece says. "I don't want to be here anymore because Mom didn't get the rain ponchos."

I stare at the wet steps and sigh. I knew that a Caroline Taylor birthday party could never be this good. I just wanted to have a good time and now

I'm stuck in the rain with a bunch of unhappy people. I'm starting to wish I'd have just stayed home.

The groundskeepers begin to lay out the tarp around the diamond. Many people take this as thinking that they game's over, but the sprinkles die down and the tarp just indicates that they need to make sure that the baseball field doesn't get too wet and muddy.

"How do I get people to stop leaving?" I think out loud.

"What," Jackie starts to laugh. "Are you going to go stand by the gate or something?"

"Yes!" I shout and run up the stairs all the way through the sitting sections. I make it to the front without getting knocked over. I go to the very front where people are starting to come in and some are starting to leave.

Behind me are Jackie and Caroline soaked and it looks like someone with ketchup ran into Caroline. "You owe me," her words come out chipped and sour.

"You can't leave," I assure a boy exiting the park with his dad. He looks at me curiously and I ignore him. "You can't miss this,"

"It's raining," He snaps.

"Uh, whatever, suit yourself." I say back. "This is never going to work."

"At least the rain is stopping," Jackie comments and just as she says that the rain comes pouring down worse than anything I've ever seen before. I almost cry, this is the worst day ever!

"Hey, Alex," Caroline pats my arm. "Just so you know, there's no crying in baseball." I smile at her and start to tap my feet.

"Happy Birthday to you," I sing and dance. "Happy Birthday to you, happy birthday dear Caroline. Happy Birthday to you!" A person walking out throws a dollar to me.

"Keep it," I hand it back. "I want everyone to stay at the game!" He takes back the dollar and walks back into the stadium. Proud, I restart my birthday song. Caroline hums along this time through. I make it so a few more people stay; a lot of them just ignore me.

By the time it's time for the game to start, it's still pouring, but Mrs. Taylor makes us sit back down anyway. The announcer says he has to say something so we wait and listen.

"Singing the national anthem, Miss Alexandria Waters," The announcing voice says.

"Huh!" I shout and turn back to Mrs. Taylor who nods. I make my way down to the diamond having Caroline and Jackie follow me. "I'm so scared!" I whisper to them.

The rain begins to pour down hard so hard that it's hard to see. My blue sweatshirt gets soaked and drenches me. I open my eyes and start to sing. "O say can you see,"

I sing all the way through with every one of the soaked fans humming along with me.

"And the home of the brave," I end the song.

Jackie and Caroline tug on me to give me hugs and the audience claps. I smile and smile and smile without ever taking my eyes away from the crowd. I want to remember this.

"Thank you," I say into the microphone and just like that the rain dies down and everyone stays to enjoy the wonderful game.

But it's not so wonderful.

We lose the game, but not by a lot.

By the time we get out of the stadium it's past midnight, but Cece insists on us eating cake at the bakery so we drive over there.

"Presenting," Cece says while Mrs. Taylor covers Caroline's eyes to make sure that she doesn't look. "The fruit-roll up peanut butter cake, aka the Caroline."

"Oh my goodness!" Caroline cries.

I make a face at Cece's cake. It has fruit roll ups on the corners of it and has this peanut butter frosting that she's been telling us about. It sounds gross, but I haven't tried it before so I don't know. It's just plain chocolate in the cake with more peanut butter moose in the middle.

"Here," Mrs. Taylor says handing me a piece. I take a bite and sigh. I didn't think it would be, but it's the best piece of cake ever. I want some for my birthday.

Rosie's missing out by going to her spy party at Gwen's.

Rosie

Sydney and I walk right behind Gwen, who is making us hold her books today as she struts down the hall like a supermodel. I take a glance over my shoulder and see Alex, Caroline, and Jackie talking and laughing without me. I sigh. I haven't talked to them in days. When I started being friends with Gwen they stopped talking to me. I didn't understand at first, but Sydney and Gwen said they were probably just jealous.

I didn't mean to ditch them on Caroline's birthday, but I how was I supposed to say no to Gwen? I couldn't and besides Gwen threw a really nice party for me. She told me it was just a spa day, but once I arrived, it was a surprise going away party for me. It was so sweet.

Today they haven't said a word to me. Caroline and them I mean. They think I ditched them for Gwen. I try really hard to apologize, but they always ignore me.

"Rosie," whispers Sydney. "Are you thinking about them again?" She asks me. I shake my head. I've noticed that Gwen doesn't like me thinking about them whatsoever. She hates them, naturally.

"How far away is your next class?" wonders Gwen.

"I'm in your next class, English," I say.

"Oh ok, great! That way you can take my books there,"

I sigh. I'm the bag lady for Gwen, that's not a big accomplishment in life.

"Okay," I reply. I've learned to follow all of Gwen's orders. So does Sydney. She thinks she's boss around school and to us, she is boss.

For most of class I just daydream. I didn't say anything to anyone, but tomorrow my dad and I are leaving for Paris to see my mom. I keep trying to tell Caroline, Alex, and Jackie, but they keep ignoring me because I didn't go to that birthday party.

Jackie, who sits in front of me in English, is writing down a bunch of things in her notebook. I'm not taking any notes, so I must not be paying much attention. I pass her a note when Ms. Cardwell isn't looking. Jackie opens the note and throws it in her binder.

I wait and wait and wait for her to answer the note, but she doesn't. It's trapped in her binder now and she's not going to look at it, she's still mad at me.

"Jackie!" I chase her down the hallway when class is done, she continues ignoring me, pretending that I'm not shouting her name and Caroline's and Alex's. "Please, listen to me!"

"What do you want?" whispers Caroline in a stern voice. I whip my head around to see her. I want to say sorry, but when she talks to me like that I don't. I start to turn in the other direction, but I soon remember why I was shouting in the first place.

"Okay," I say, remaining calm. "I really am sorry for ditching you on your birthday and I didn't want to hurt your feelings."

"So why didn't you come?" snaps Alex.

"Because I was at Gwen's party," I answer her in her same tone of voice.

"How in the world is stupid Gwen Biggley's party better than Caroline's?" asks Jackie.

"It wasn't stupid!" I shout at them. "It was actually MY party! It was for me! She threw me a going away party because I'm the one leaving and she cared about it."

"I doubt that Gwen cared about you, since when has she cared about anyone?" Alex says in a mean tone. I glare at her.

"Anyway, I'm sorry." I say. "I didn't mean to ditch you on your birthday, Caroline." I give her the gift card I got her and meant to give her the other day.

"It's okay,"

"I'm moving tomorrow," I tell them. "I'm so sorry I didn't give you further notice or anything so we could have like a going away party with us, but you were all so mad at me. I didn't have a chance until now."

"Oh," Caroline whispers. "Coach Ruth wanted me to give this to you."

I open the piece of paper she hands to me.

Dear Rosie,
Good luck in Paris with your mom and dad and the rest of your family. The Baseball Club for Girls isn't going to be the same without you. Sure, we had

*a practice and a half, but we've
gotten to know you very well
and know that one day we'll
see you on TV coaching your
own baseball club.*
Love,
*Coach Ruth and Coach Jim
Keener*
Ruth and Jim Keener

I tuck the message in my pocket and eye everyone curiously. I didn't want Coach Ruth and Coach Jim to know that I was moving. I didn't want them to kick me off the team and this note is clearly kicking me off and somebody told them.

"Who said anything to Coach Ruth and Coach Jim about me moving?" I ask them. Everyone is quiet for a second. "I didn't say anything to them." I remind them.

"I told Coach Ruth and Coach Jim that you might be moving," Alex says. "I didn't say that you were."

"But someone did," I say.

"Me," whispers Caroline. "I was upset that day at practice that you weren't there and I said that it wouldn't matter because in a couple of months or weeks you wouldn't even be there."

"Wait, how did you know when I was moving?" I ask.

"I didn't," Caroline replies. "Ruth wrote it after I told her you'd be moving. I held on to it so I could give it to you whenever you moved."

"Oh," I say. I don't have any more words for them.

I grab my stuff and head to lunch, my last lunch that is, here at least. I hate the fact that I have to say that. For months I've been waiting to move and now it's here and I don't want to. Paris seems so far away and it is, but I wish it wasn't. Just when I when I get my friends back I'm losing them again.

"Why on Earth were you talking to them?" Gwen asks. I look down at my food. I don't want to start a conversation right now. I just want to relax, which I obviously won't get to do.

I instead take in my last lunch at Riverside Waters Middle School. It's a shame that I have to eat my last lunch here with Gwen and Sydney. I'd rather be talking with Caroline, Alex, and Jackie, but I can't,

Gwen controls the power of who can and who can't sit with her and I'm forced to. So I can't sit with them.

***

I throw down my backpack and sit on the couch. Bags and packed up and ready to go. My dad is still in his office, probably adjusting last minute things and making another list so the neighbors know what stuff to mail us in a couple of weeks. Including Sundae, who is staying with the neighbors.

I get up and check my bedroom for items I might have missed, but I didn't miss anything, my room just looks sad and empty, just as it looked when my mother picked it out when we moved in here and I swore I never wanted to live in this house. Now it's what's most important to me.

The walls a pale pink are all faded and the shelves hanging upside down. My closet, none of my clothes on any of the hangers. Instead in big brown boxes packed away.

I rip open a box with pictures in it and find the one with my mom and me when we moved in here. She was about to go back to Paris, but she wanted to find us a house first. It was the saddest day of my life when Mom left for Paris.

Mom hasn't visited the house in a while. The last she saw of it was that day and even then the house wasn't clean and perfect and didn't have that amazing Dawkins twist on it.

I can hardly imagine a home in Paris, France more relaxing and more special than this one. Mom has a lot to live up to.

"Ready to go, Rosie?" asks Dad. I turn my head and shut off the bedroom light. I nod my head and leave the room, forever.

Offseason

"I might not be in Paris, but I'm somewhere,"

Rosie

"Can I help you?" asks the counter lady at the airport. My dad hands her our tickets and she checks our bags. "Paris I see," She comments on our tickets. "I assume you're not going to world premiere of 'The Little Tea Shop'."

"Starring who?" I wonder.

"Adelynn Simone of course," The lady replies. "I heard that movie is amazing." Her voice looses it's prep and her gaze falters.

"I didn't know she was in another movie," I say to my dad. He looks at me cautiously, blinking furiously.

"We're going to see Ms. Simone," My dad explains to the lady. She smiles at him. "Wait -, are you Julia Davy?"

The counter lady nods her head. "Oh my, you're Victor Dawkins! Wow, I didn't know you were interested in Adelynn Simone's movies. You never were when we were in school. You thought she was a snob."

"Then I asked her to senior prom," Dad laughs. "We're actually married now." The counter lady pretends to gasp.

"I knew it would happen someday, you two hated each other until you had to hang out together, oh but when that day happened it was so meant to be." Julia, the lady, says.

My dad and Julia Davy laugh on and on about high school memories. I guess Dad is uncomfortable being all by himself (with me, I think angrily) and Julia misses the good old days in high school. I take my turn rolling my eyes and sighing.

"Wow," Julia says looking at our tickets again. "Victor Dawkins and daughter moving to Paris, France, that's so unlike you."

"Well, I want to see Adelynn and so does Rosie." He puts his hand on my shoulder, I shrug away.

"Hello, I'm Julia Davy," Julia shakes my hand.

"I'm Rosie Dawkins," I say, shaking back with no emotion in my voice.

"Wow," snorts Julia. "I always thought that the one thing Adelynn would take is her name. I thought for sure you would be a Simone."

I shake my head.

"Nope," Dad says. "She's a Dawkins," Julia and Dad exchange numbers and we walk away to board the airplane. I throw him an angry glance.

"Who was she?" I snap. Mom might be a few thousand miles away, but she's still Mom and not this Julia Davy baggage airport stupid lady person.

"That, my Rosie pie, was Julia Davy." He says. "The last girlfriend before Adelynn, I mean, Mommy." I glare at him. "Oh come on, Rosie. Julia Davy is a nice girl. Are you telling me I can't even say hi to my friends?"

"Not Julia Davy," I snap. "I don't want Julia to ever replace Mom. In case you forgot she's still married to you." I remind him.

He starts to laugh. "Rosie, Julia and I are friends. Mom and Julia were friends too and then, there was some issues and fighting with them, but they're grown adults, Ro."

"Whatever," I say.

My dad checks his phone and listens to a voicemail from Mom. I stare back over at Julia Davy. So Mom had to get through Julia Davy before she was a superstar and had dad. I never would have guessed, I always assumed she was always popular.

"Come on Rosie," Dad tugs my arm back to the front desk, where he throws our plane tickets.

"What are you doing?" I cry.

Julia looks back over at us. "Is everything okay?" She asks. "Do you need your tickets? I think you need those to get on the airplane." She starts to laugh.

Dad starts talking to Julia again, only this time about NOT going to Paris. He says that Mom didn't really mean to invite us to Paris to live, but only to tell us about her new movie release.

"What?" I cry. Julia and Dad stare. I stare them down. Dad is mad at Mom and now he's reuniting with Julia Davy. This is the worst day ever.

"I knew that she didn't want us to ruin her career," My dad vents.

"I found this," Julia pulls out a magazine. "It has an interview with her about her movie."

"The Little Tea Shop" hits theaters!
The Little Tea Shop, starring

Adelynn Simone is hitting the big screens November 18th.

The story revolves around movie star, Gina Andrews (Simone) and her retired parents (Julia Young & Darwin Peters) who own a tea shop that is shutting down due to bad business. In search for help, Gina calls to America for her husband (Ryan Hank) and daughter (Peyton Scraper).

"I think the movie is amazing," says Adelynn Simone, superstar and lead actress. "I want everyone to enjoy this movie as much as I do."

"Adelynn is awesome to work with," Ryan Hank comments on his wife in the movie. "She's so much fun."

"Adelynn is like a mom to me," Peyton Scraper says. "She's so good at her job."

The Little Tea Shop hits theaters November 18th.

A tear slides down my cheek. I hand the magazine back to Julia. Dad and I look at each other and I sigh again, tears dripping down my face.

"She didn't want us in Paris," I say, sniffling through the many tears. Dad and Julia just stare at me again without any talking. I just want to go home now. It isn't fair, this isn't fair.

"I sure would like to talk some sense into Adelynn someday." Julia says. "I bet she hasn't changed,"

"Uh, please don't. Rosie pie chill, I have to use the restroom." Dad walks away to the bathroom.

Julia starts to laugh when he walks away. "What's so funny?" I ask.

"Nothing, it's just that I've known your parents since I was in second grade and now I know their daughter," She sighs. "I can't believe they got married. It seemed like such a tossup in high school."

"What?" I ask, curious. I thought she said my mom and dad were meant to be.

"Nothing," She replies as my dad comes back. "Your daughter is so nice," She says to him.

"We should catch up again sometime," Dad says taking our suitcases to the car. He doesn't sound serious.

"Oh yeah," Julia nods. She helps us out. "I would really like that," I wouldn't, I think to myself.

"That was nice," Dad says as we get in the car.

"You still like Julia, right?" I ask.

"Not at all," My dad replies. "I was just being nice, but there are a few reasons that I broke up with her. She might have a different opinion, but I was just being nice."

"Okay," I say. "She seemed weird,"

"Nah," Dad says. "She just wanted to catch up, it was so dramatic in high school with your mom and her and I."

"I can tell," I snort.

"Thank you, Rosie." Dad turns his head back at me. "You were very good today."

I smile. I might not be in Paris, but I'm somewhere.

Jackie

"It's freezing!" complains Alex. It seems as if she never stops complaining, but I'm with her. My grandma is making us practice in the snow.

"Alright, alright, wrap it up." Grandma says, packing up the bats and helmets. I walk with Alex and Caroline to the inside of the REC center to buy hot chocolate. That's been our daily thing if it's cold outside.

"Have you heard anymore from Rosie?" Caroline asks. I shake my head. A few days ago, Rosie called us and said that she wasn't moving to Paris. She said that her mom was actually saying the plot of a movie when she invited them and now her mom and dad are arguing. She also said that her dad was talking to this Julia Davy person that her mom hates and that's making them fight more. How did she not tell the difference between a movie and an invitation?

Even though Rosie isn't moving, she doesn't want to come back to the team yet. I guess because she quit she doesn't think she is welcome back, but my grandma said that she was.

"Rosie texted me last night," Alex says. "She can come to tryouts tomorrow. I do not want to go to that." Alex has to do a music video for the school board. Her dad wants her to hold auditions and start doing the music video. She wants Caroline, Rosie, and I to be in it, but I can't sing or dance at all.

Grandma had to cancel practice for tomorrow because Alex has to hold tryouts. Grandma's sad about canceling, but we can't do anything anyway. I do not want to practice in the snow and neither does the rest of the team.

"We need to start fundraisers now," Grandma said to me last night. "We need to be doing something; we can't just take a break." I agree with her, but Alex, Caroline, Rosie, and I are almost teenager girls, we like to do other things in our spare time too.

"I'm so mad about tomorrow," groans Alex.

"Stop your whining," Grandma says sarcastically. "You don't have to come to baseball practice, aren't you happy?"

Alex showed us the signup sheet and she has a reason to be so mad. Not only did Sydney Mister and stupid Gwen Biggley sign up, but so did a mixture of nerds, Pon Pom girls, cheerleaders, populars, and more.

"I'd rather practice in the snow and rain," Alex replies. I didn't want to go to the auditions at first, but now Alex is forcing Caroline, Rosie, and I to go. She doesn't want to do this alone.

**

"I'm home," I say to Grandpa, who is sitting on the couch snoring. It's good that we have kids like Murray and Junior at the foster home because Grandpa isn't always paying attention.

I head to the kitchen to grab a snack and then head to my room. I do the same routine every day. I eat my snack in my room and do my homework. When I'm done I take a shower and curl my hair. I feel like I need to clean myself after being at stinky baseball practice.

I have to admit, I didn't think that the baseball club for girls was going to be this fun. Rosie and I thought about the club that day after school. I didn't think this it would ever work, but it did. I used to play with the boys, whenever they were missing someone, but it wasn't the same. With this it's better, because I can mess up and not feel stupid. We all are learning at the same time.

"I made cookies," Murray comes into my room with a tray of cookies and milk. Murray and I have gotten along better since my dad left. She was jealous and I was jealous too. She was jealous because I had a dad and she didn't and I was jealous because she was jealous. Grandma and Grandpa talked to us and told us to stop acting like we hated each other and start acting like sisters.

"Thanks," I say. I take a cookie and a glass of milk.

I finish my homework really quickly and decide to work on some ideas for the music video auditions. I fall asleep while trying to think and before I know it it's tomorrow.

***

"I'm not looking forward to this," Caroline mumbles looking at the bleachers. Not a lot of people showed up, but enough showed up to make a video.

"Should I just go in alphabetical order?" Alex asks, looking at her signup clipboard.

"Yeah," whispers Rosie.

"Okay," Alex says. "Here we go, Genevieve Biggley?"

"I'm here!" shouts Gwen in her purple ruffle tutu skirt and leopard print sunglasses. She runs down to the front of our table and glares. "I didn't know you guys were helping lame Waters hold auditions," She says to Caroline and me. "And I thought you were supposed be in Paris with your famous mom, Rosie."

Stunned, Rosie looks down at the ground. Ever since Rosie's been back at school since her 'last day' Gwen and everyone else has been super mean to her and calling her a liar because she said that she has a mom that is an actress in Paris. Nobody believes her.

"I can tell the difference between a superstar and a stupid liar." Gwen sasses, turning away.

"Are you going to tryout or just tease because we don't have all day?" I snap.

"Please," Caroline adds.

"Whatever," Gwen says. "I'm going to sing and dance at the same time. I'm multitalented like that."

"Okay,"

"Oh…I was scared that night because the shoe store man was a fright; he scared me with his buck teeth and stinky cheese breath. I thought I might just

116

die, when I saw a cat out my window that very night. It was a scary thing and I started to cry.

"Oh why, aye, do you make me eat that fast food? I don't like McDonald's or Burger King anymore! I don't want to eat that gross fast food. Just like all my scares, it will scare me there. No more, no more fast food or cats, or shoe store owners."

She bows after ridiculous dance moves are thrown in there. She mostly just kicks up and twirls. By the time she finishes we're all crying.

"I know, I know, it was that good." She takes another bow. "Now, I can burn you a CD if you like it that much." She takes out a CD and throws it on the table.

"Uh, did you write that?" asks Alex.

"Duh, who else would?" Gwen snaps.

"We'll get back to you." Rosie pretends to smile.

"What?" She screams. "I wrote a very true sad song about my deepest fears and I have to deal with a 'back to you'. Yeah, no, I'm in."

"Maybe a backup dancer," Caroline tries to cheer her up. Caroline Taylor is too nice to tell her that she stinks.

"Sure," Alex nods. "That might work, thanks Gwen see you tomorrow."

Gwen runs away screaming her head off and demanding that she's the lead. I roll my eyes.

"Disaster," Rosie starts to laugh when Gwen is out of sight. "I can't believe we're doing this,"

None of the rest of the auditions lives up to Gwen's, but a few of them are good.

We might have an 'okay' music video.

Caroline

"A delayed flight?" I turn my head to face my mom, who is talking to my dad. I start to panic and flash a glance at my siblings, who are intently listening to my mom's every words just like I am. This Thanksgiving isn't going to be any better than my birthday was.

My birthday was amazing, I'm not trying to say it was bad, but without my dad here now and without him here on Thanksgiving the two are about to be the same.

"Where's Daddy?" Ashley and Cody say at the same time. My mom shushes them and continues talking to my dad. I look at Cece, who looks very interested in her mashed potatoes. I try to look into mine, but all I see is my dad, his favorite food is mashed potatoes.

Mom hangs up the phone and sighs. I know that he's not going to be home for Thanksgiving either.

"That was Dad," Mom says. "There's uh, snowstorm and his flight can't take off so he won't be home until Saturday."

"That's TWO days after Thanksgiving!" shouts Cody.

"That's no fair! Bad snow!" screams Ashley.

"I know," Mom sighs. "I want him home for Thanksgiving too." Cece doesn't look up from her mashed potatoes, Mom and I stare at her. This is usually when she brings up everyone's spirits and has Cody and Ashley do some sort of craft.

But Cece doesn't perk up and she doesn't say anything. She just stares at her dinner and starts to cry.

"Cece," Mom whispers. "What's wrong?"

"Dad knows that Thanksgiving is my most favorite holiday of the year and he won't be home in time! That's not fair!" She shouts.

"Hmm," Mom says. "That reminds me of a few weeks ago, when someone else would have the same feeling. They were much more upset than you, and had a very good reason to be."

"Who are you talking about?" snaps Cece.

"Caroline," Mom replies. "Don't you remember, Caroline's birthday and Daddy wasn't home."

"Whatever," Cece sighs. "He should just be here so we don't have to be upset."

I agree with her, but she doesn't have to be so mean about it.

***

Black Friday is one of the busiest days of the year in our house. We all kind of split up and shop. Mom gets up super early, like four, to go shopping and Cece goes with her. Normally, Cody, Ashley, and I have to go to Grandma's and at like noon she takes us to Midnight Sweets.

Instead, this year Coach Ruth and Coach Jim want us to have a bake sale at Midnight Sweets all day to raise money. I don't know anyone who wants a cupcake at six a.m., but we also have coffees, donuts, bagels, and more. Along with Uncle Rob's diner.

I wake up and stretch my arms out wide. The fact that I'm up at four a.m. is crazy. I never wake up this early. I grab my coat and go out the front door where Coach Ruth and Coach Jim are waiting for me. I have to just force myself up and leave. The breakfast and our 'uniforms' are at the shop.

"Good Morning, Caroline!" says Coach Jim. Jackie is already in the car.

Alex is next and then Rosie, each groaning once they sit down. "I hate mornings." Alex whines.

At the bakery, we put on our uniforms that Rosie picked out. She got us pink tutu skirts and blue t-shirts with our last names on the back of them. My reads 'Taylor' and on my tutu skirt it says 'Caroline' in the corner. The outfit is super cute and my aunt Reba offers to braid our hair.

"Aw!" Aunt Reba says once we're finished. "That's amazing, y'all look fabulous." She takes a picture and prints it out on her automatic printer. She writes our names on it and hangs it in the window along with our donation sign that Jackie made.

We even have a signup sheet in case anyone else wants to sign up since we only have four of us.

"I've just started some coffee and I have some donuts and bagels in the back set aside for y'all." Aunt Reba continues. "Try not to snack on too many sweets and I'll tell you when you can start to make some more."

"How cool!" beams Rosie, twirling around in her pink tutu. "I want to make a 'Rosie' cupcake, that's what I'm going to call it. Sweet, huh?" 'Sweet' is a bit much, but it's still funny and fun at this early in the morning.

"I'm bored," Alex complains. "Nobody is coming."

"That is because," My aunt laughs. "We aren't open, yet."

"Whatever," groans Alex, obviously embarrassed. "When do we open?"

"Right about now," Aunt Reba answers. "This town knows what time on Black Friday to come around. Don't you worry at all, I know my costumers and they like their sweets. By the way, this is also my husband's diner." My uncle Rob waves from across the room. "Today you are waitresses. Put on these aprons."

She hands us pink aprons to put on. They all have our names on them.

"Here come some people, girls. Get ready!" My aunt Reba absolutely adores the day after Thanksgiving. She says it's her busiest sales day and so much fun. I can tell by the way she jumps when somebody come in.

"Hello," Alex, Rosie, and Jackie chorus when the people come in. They stare at me curiously. I didn't talk, I'm super shy, but by the way they're looking at me, I know I'm going to have to say the rest.

Rosie hands me the script with our donation papers. "Uh, hi," I begin.

"Good morning." A man says, behind him is a lady. The two of them look irritated and tired.

"I'm Rosie Dawkins," Rosie takes over. "This is Alex Waters, Jackie Heaters, and Caroline Taylor. This is our Baseball Club, for girls. We were wondering if you'd donate."

"What's the purpose of this?"demands the lady.

"Um, there aren't any girl sports teams – besides cheer and pom – and we want to play baseball." Alex continues.

"We're having this fundraiser to raise money for bats and helmets and we want to sign up to be a team. We need a lot more people too." Jackie explains.

"Yeah," I mumble. Why am I so shy?

124

"Deals, girls, make deals." I hear my aunt demand behind her desk. I nod and so do the rest of them. Alex looks at me to say something, but I'm too shy to.

"Did you know how delicious and amazing these cakes are? I know the people who work make them and they are amazing also!" exclaims Rosie in the cheesiest voice ever. She grabs a 'sweet lovers' cupcake and shoves it in her mouth. The sweet cupcakes are so sugary and sweet that her eyes start to water. She coughs the treat back up.

"Uh," I say in a rush of panic. "It's like five a.m. and those cupcakes are SO sweet, um, you love that right, Ro?" I turn my body towards Rosie. Alex and Jackie are patting Rosie's back to make sure the cake isn't stuck in her throat.

"Yummy," coughs Rosie. "Yeah, you should buy some, but don't eat them right now, they're, uh, too sweet now."

My aunt Reba shakes her head in disbelief.

"Okay, I just want someone to seat me." The lady complains.

"Right this way," Uncle Rob takes the lady's hand, the man following behind.

"ROB!" screeches Aunt Reba in a whisper. "This is the girl's job, let them wait on them."

Jackie, Alex, Rosie, and I stand up and take the menus.

"Hi, I'm Rosie Dawkins, I will be your server today, and would you like a beverage?"

"No thanks," The man says.

"Water please," replies the lady.

"Water, okay. Do you want to look at the menu for a second?"

"Yeah,"

Rosie walks away and we all look around.

"This is boring," Alex cries. "One costumer, they look bored. We need entertainment."

"Uh, Alex," Rosie taps her. "It's only five a.m. In case you haven't noticed. WE ARE ALL BORED!"

"If you want entertainment then why don't you do something?" asks Jackie.

"Okay," Alex moans.

Alex gets on top of one of the tables and starts to dance and twirl a little bit. My uncle cringes once he sees her on top of the table. It takes a long time to wash those.

"Sing," shouts Rosie.

Alex turns back to us with bright pink cheeks. She turns her body towards the window, where a bunch of people have gathered.

"KEEP DANCING!" shouts Aunt Reba.

Alex does as told and jazzes it up a bit. Aunt Reba starts to play her guitar, which gets Alex dancing more. Laughing, I twirl around.

"SING!" shouts Jackie.

"SING!" I shout.

"Okay, okay, join me." Alex laughs.

"This is Midnight Sweets," Alex sings to go with the country music. "Home of the world's most yummy treats/I want to live here/it's full of love and cheer/"

"SING ABOUT SOMETHING ELSE!" Aunt Reba shouts. "What about you? Why are you here?"

My aunt puts away the music.

Alex sits down on the table and looks at the crowd who has lined up inside now to watch her. "I want donations, just for a special cause."

"Ooh," Rosie, Jackie, and I sing.

"I'm selling sweets to work in that summer heat I want to play like the boys that play to the postseason and work to throw a perfect game." She speeds up the music and starts to dance. "You want me to dance in a tutu skirt and show off and be a big fat jerk, but I'm sorry I want to play ball."

"I might be small!" shouts Rosie in a sing-song voice.

"Do-do-do," I back up.

"I might be tall!" Jackie sings.

"Do-do-do,"

"THE BASEBALL CLUB!" I scream. "FOR GIRLS!"

We repeat and add more with people screaming for us to do more. They want to eat too and make donations.

"Do you think I could sing Christmas songs?" asks Alex, obviously absorbed in the magic of people screaming and shouting from more out of us.

"Of course," My aunt Reba says.

The sales die down after a while and we decide to cut down on the music. The Christmas music in the afternoon drives people crazy and Alex even suggests going outside to draw people in. Rosie, Jackie, and I are super cold and want to go back in, but Alex won't leave so she continues to sing. We get tons more people to come in.

"Wow," My mom says when she comes in, after shopping for a few hours. "I was at the store across the street and someone said that Midnight Sweets was amazing today, they had the most talented little girls and great baked goods."

"That's amazing!" Rosie squeals.

My mom comes over to talk to me. "Your dad is on his way home," She says in a whisper. My face brightens up and I smile. "So, did you make a lot of money?" She asks Aunt Reba.

"I think this has been the most money we've made on Black Friday." My aunt replies.

"Look Mommy!"

A little girl is pointing and screaming at Rosie and me.

"Oh I'm so sorry," The girl's mother says. "My son saw you girls earlier this morning and thought this was really cool. He said you girls are trying to save a Tea Shop?"

"Save a tea shop?" My mom laughs. "No this is a baseball fundraiser."

"I picked up a newspaper and it says right here that today is a fundraiser to say McBerry Diner." The woman continues. "Isn't your mom in Paris?" she asks Rosie.

"Uh, yeah." Rosie replies shaking.

"It says that you and your dad need money to save a tea shop and raise money to go to Paris. Elise, right?"

"My name is Rosie Dawkins," Rosie's voice slows down and trails off. "I'm not saving any tea shop."

"Your mom is Gina?"

"No," Rosie replies, sounding scared. "My mom's name is Adelynn Simone, she's an actress."

"An actress?" the lady exclaims. "That's not what this says. Why don't you read this?" I hand the paper to my mom, who reads it carefully.

"Reba," She calls to my aunt. "Didn't you send in an article to the newspaper?" My aunt peers over the front desk and nods. "Why'd you say we were supporting a tea shop?"

"Tea shop?" laughs Aunt Reba. "I didn't say nothing about a tea shop. I saw an awful movie 'bout a tea shop."

"My mom was in a movie about a tea shop," says Rosie lightly.

"The Little Tea Shop?" asks Aunt Reba. Rosie nods. "I say, waste of time, sorry."

My mom takes another look at the article. "We don't need to make a big deal about this, I'm sorry ma'am, but we aren't saving a tea shop, we're doing just fine. Thank you."

"Mommy, can I have a cookie?" The girl asks.

"Sure, sweetie," I hand her a cookie with a flower on it and she smiles. "I'm sure the newspaper was just putting movie reviews in the news section. I mean, who puts a baseball club fundraiser in the critic's corner."

"That's us," Aunt Reba says. "That was us, not the tea shop. Thank you for stopping by." The little girl and her mom leave and I sigh.

"That was weird," I say.

"What was weird?" asks Jackie, coming from the back room.

"Yeah, what happened?" wonders Alex, since she was outside.

"Never mind," Aunt Reba laughs.

Rosie

"We're heading to the airport at four, okay?" My dad says to me when I wake up. It's the day of the Santa Land parade and my mom is coming into town to watch and then she has a bunch of talk shows to star in. I'm stressed out, my dad is stressed out, it's a big rush of stress in this house and on top of that I have to perform in the parade with Caroline, Jackie, and Alex. According to the town of Riverside, we're the little Tea Shop Girls.

My mom has been planning her trip to Riverside since August and people are already at the parade to see her make her appearance. She never mentioned her visit to my dad until a few days ago and now Dad has to get the house ready.

After the problem with the airport and Julia Davy, my dad has been mad at my mom because she wasn't clear enough with the visit planning.

"Victor," My mom had said. I was eavesdropping on their video chat that night. "There wouldn't have been time to visit anyway. You're so silly."

"Silly?" my dad had screamed. "I thought I was moving to Paris."

133

That was the end of that and now they've been pretty silent. I'm not exactly thrilled to have here all week because I know that she's going to be bombarded with questions and I won't get to see her.

Once we arrive at the airport news crews are setting up before we are and smiling at us and waving their hands for us to come near.

"How big of a fan are you of Adelynn Simone?" asks a news man to Julia Davy, who is standing at her front desk. She looks around and gives us a look of sympathy.

"Uh, I'm a fan, I went to high school with her." replies Julia.

"How famous was she then?"

"Uh, we were friends, she wasn't famous. I liked her better that way." Julia flashes a smile at my dad and me. "I wonder how her life is now."

"So did you go to high school in Paris?"

"No," Julia laughs. "Adelynn went to Riverside Waters High School, just like I did. She wasn't born a star."

"Thank you, uh, who are you?" asks the news crew.

"Julia Davy,"

Julia rolls her eyes when they walk away. That interview was awful and it must have been worse to have to answer the questions. Nobody seems to ask me who I am; I'm starting to think that maybe the world doesn't know that Adelynn Simone has a daughter, which is worrying me.

"Here she comes!" Daniel May, the newscaster on Channel 2 Riverside news shouts. As soon as he says two words, the cameras are shining on my mom who is slowly making her way off the plane.

"Hello, Ms. Simone, how does do you like Riverside?" Daniel May asks.

"I just got off the plane," Mom laughs. "But I grew up here and I remember how many memories I have here." She hugs my father. "This is my husband, he lives here and I wish I could have him with me in Paris."

"Who is this?" Camera Crew people push me towards my mom and ask her repeatedly who I am. I try to smile at the camera and my mom, but the people around me are squeezing me.

"A fan, probably." My mom replies. "What do I sign? I have to get to the Santa Land Parade."

"I'm not a fan," I snap.

"A hater?" Daniel asks.

"Uh, I'm your daughter!" I shout. She stands back and starts to laugh.

"I had a four year old, but we gave her up for adoption eight years ago." My mom explains to the press. My dad looks uncomfortable and tries to avoid the spotlight.

"No!" I yell. My whole face gets red and I start to heat up. "You never gave me up! I'm Rosie Dawkins, your daughter!"

My mom, whom I should just call Adelynn, turns to the camera with a face of pure disgust. I start to cry. My own mother thinks she put me up for adoption and why would she even want to? How can she not remember?

I stick my hand in my pocket and take out the picture of us when I was four. I hand it to her and go to the front desk with Julia; I never thought that I'd turn to her right now.

She just stares at the cameras and news and sighs. "You know," Julia says sadly. "I never thought in a million years that Adelynn Simone would do that. She was my friend and nice, but now, I don't even know her or your dad."

I sigh.

"Come on, Rosie." Dad comes over and yanks my arm. He yanks me all the way to the car. I've never seen Dad so angry as he makes the cameras leave us alone. Mom, on the other hand, waves to the cameras and announces her appearance on the news tomorrow morning.

"Okay," Dad raises his voice. "No cameras, no more people, got it? Adelynn, this is Rosie, don't act like you don't have a daughter and no we didn't say adoption at all."

Mom is silent she looks at the picture I handed her again. I didn't realize how incredibly fake she is. She's just a snobby actress who only worries about herself. I don't know why I thought she was my mom, a real mom.

"You said when that foster home opened you were putting her up." She replies.

"Yeah, it opened eight years ago and then I knew I wasn't making her go through that because you didn't want a kid in your life." Dad snaps back. "Why do you think we're going to that parade?"

"Because people want to see me," Mom answers.

"Rosie's in the parade! It's a kid parade and in America, not everyone knows who you are." Dad tells her. She rolls her eyes.

***

"This is ridiculous," I turn my head and look at the program that Jackie is holding. "Why are we Tea Shop Girls again?" she wonders.

"Um, duh, we saved a tea shop!" Alex says sarcastically.

"What does that have to do with Christmas?" I ask, laughing. That tea shop article was so funny. They mixed up the reviews and our fundraiser article up so now everyone wants us to be some musical group in the Santa Land parade.

We assigned Alex to the Christmas singing and Caroline, Jackie, and I are background dancers on the float, which is shaped like a giant tea shop.

"I have no idea," Alex continues laughing putting a Santa hat on my head. She dances around in her skirt and lip syncs into the microphone to the Christmas song that's on.

"So, how's your mom?" Caroline changes the subject in a quiet voice. Alex stops and Jackie turns around to face me. I look at the ground and over at Alex.

"When is your brother coming home again?" I wonder, trying desperately not to have to talk about my mom before the big parade. I don't want to be sad when I have to spread all this Christmas cheer.

"He's flying in tomorrow, but he's not coming to stay until Christmas Eve." answers Alex. "I can't wait!"

I stare at the floor again. I thought that I couldn't wait and now I'd rather be living in that stupid orphanage than my real home with my snotty mom who doesn't care about me. I would explain her to my friends, but not now, they won't understand until they meet her.

The five minute warning for the parade to start is called out. Jackie hands out the finished Santa hats, full with glitter and a cotton ball at the end.

"Now presenting to you the Santa Land parade Riverside Waters 2011!" The announcer announces and smiles at everyone. We start our routine as we pass by the food court on carts. Alex begins 'Winter Wonderland' as Jackie, Caroline, and I pretend to be serving Alex tea.

Coach Ruth and Coach Jim are sitting by my dad, Murray and Junior, and Caroline's family. Alex's family was too busy to come see her in the parade, but I don't think she really wanted them to come and ruin her big moment.

My mom is watching up and down the streets and screaming and dancing to the music that Alex is singing. I try not to stare because my friends don't know what my mom looks like and I don't want them to know that that's her.

"Is that your mom?" whispers Jackie pointing down at her. She's directing the floats to move and is dancing with an elf up and down the street. I look down and start to cringe. Why did I want to be related to a famous actress so bad? She doesn't make life easier, just harder.

"Yes," I mumble and start dancing to Rock'n around the Christmas tree.

"The Tea Shop Girls!" The announcer presents us to the ground. "These 'sweet as tea' girls are sponsoring The Baseball Club for Girls. They are Caroline Taylor, Alex Waters, Rosie Dawkins, and Jackie Heaters."

Coach Ruth and Coach Jim wave at us as our float drives by. My mom looks up at me when the float passes by. My dad points to me and she nods. I think she mouths 'baseball' or something like that and waves. I wave too. Maybe my mom isn't all diva.

Alex

"MERRY CHRISTMAS!" I fling my arms around my brother as soon as I open the door. Not seeing him in months has made me appreciate him when he is here. His girlfriend Angela gives me a hug too and they both try to say hi to my mom and dad, who don't even turn their heads.

My parents have been trying all week to get my brother to spend Christmas Eve and Christmas with someone else. I don't understand why, since the very last time I saw him was my birthday.

"Hi, Mr. and Mrs. Waters," Angela says. They ignore her, as usual.

"Hi, Mom and Dad," My brother says. They ignore him, as usual.

Christmas around here wouldn't be any fun without him coming home. I got invited to have dinner with the Taylors, but when I found out for sure that Al was coming home I turned them down. My parents can be super stubborn anyway, so there wasn't a big chance I wasn't even going to go to that dinner anyway.

"I want to see that video you made for school," Al requests. I start to laugh. I had Jackie's brother Junior put it on DVD and the whole thing is mainly just Caroline, Rosie, Jackie, and I. I don't think that anyone else was in it. They didn't show up and they refused to listen. We had about two background dancers and one background singer.

I wrote the song when I was super bored and it mainly just covers the requirements on the paper. The video must be about education and safety and must have students that attend a Riverside Waters district school building. My dad is yet to see it, but I don't think he is going to like it.

"We should watch that tonight," Dad suggests looking up from his newspaper. I swear he reads the same newspaper every single day. That or he's an hourly subscriber.

I'm just happy that my dad actually is starting a conversation and agreeing with something that Al said. It's going to take a while longer for my mom to start, though. Mom can hold a grudge and can declare she's not going to talk to Al.

On Mother's Day, Al bought a nice card for Mom and she didn't pick up the phone once to call and thank him.

Last Christmas, he and I bought her and dad this nice microwave that she can keep in her work office and she wouldn't even thank me!

On his birthday, she called him, but not to talk to him, she wanted him to know that she wanted him to come pick up something he left there.

"What's for dinner?" I ask my mom. All day she's been busy in the kitchen making dinner. Usually she just makes soup, but because she's been using so many spices I'm hoping that maybe she made turkey or ham.

"Soup," She replies. Her voice sharp as a tack.

"I love soup," whispers Angela just loud enough for my mom to hear.

"Oh, you meant for Angela and Al, did you?" Mom continues. "They get peanut butter and anchovy sandwiches."

"Gross," I say.

"My mom used to make us anchovy and onion sandwiches all the time, I always thought they were disgusting, but I'm sure that yours with the peanut butter will be a nice touch, Mrs. W." Angela smiles.

"Sweetie," My mom shouts to my dad, ignoring my brother's girlfriend. "What time are the Biggley's coming over?"

My mouth drops open. The most awful, meanest girl in school and her family are coming over for our Christmas Eve dinner? Does Mom hate me too? I would think that she would let me enjoy my brother's company not have the absurd Biggley's over!

"Five," Dad answers. I cringe, it's nearly five.

"Isn't your friend that Gwen Biggley?" Al asks.

I shake my head.

When we were in kindergarten Gwen and I were best friends. We shared everything. First grade we were too and then in second grade there was a new girl in our class and everything changed. Jackie Heaters was the new girl. Gwen and Jackie became close friends and I was kind of abandoned. In fifth grade, Jackie's mom passed away and she got kind of independent and didn't want anyone to bother her. Gwen got offended and wanted to be my friend again, but while she was BFF's with Jackie, she was mean to me and I didn't want to be her friend again.

I told her no when she invited me to her birthday party last year and she promised me that she would make my life miserable. I would never be invited to parties in middle school, I wouldn't make any friends, I would never be popular. She actually hand wrote me a list and signed it like a document.

And all because I didn't want her to be my friend. She was awful to me, though and probably will be until I'm a grown adult.

Some people are just crazy and evil.

"Why didn't you invite the Dawkins or the Taylors or the Heaters?" I ask my mom, pleadingly. The weirdest of this is that Jackie and I are good friends now and to think she made me lose my best friend. I can't imagine that Gwen and I were friends now, she's such a snot and I bet I was when I was her friend.

"Be nice Alexandria," Mom snaps. "I want to make a good impression on another school board member family. Being president, it's hard to make a lot of close friends that are in this neighborhood.

"Mom, Jackie and her family are two houses down from us," I remind her.

"What do you want me to do? I can't make dinner for two hundred, Alex." She questions me. She does make a valid point, but still.

"What about Jackie and Ruth and Jim? They would be fun and Murray and Junior could watch the kids!"

"Foster kids watching more foster kids! They'd run away for Pete's sake! Just go get ready they are coming any minute now. We want to look nice for our house guests."

"They're already here," I point to Angela and Al, who look scared by my mom and I. I'm sick of this, though. I don't have enough patience for Gwen and her family.

I listen to my mom anyway and change and curl my hair in attempt to look nice for everyone tonight. I know what my mom was saying by making a nice impression. My parents don't make friends easily. They're super strict and not outgoing and talk about themselves whenever we have company.

"Merry Christmas 'Eve'!" screams Lauren Biggley as soon as she gets through our door. "I brought mashed potatoes and strawberry shortcake."

"Oh it's you," Gwen snorts when I come from the dining room.

"This is my house," I smart mouth her so she seems stupid. She ignores me and instead inspects my house. She seems to inspect my brother too and with one look I know she's my competition for the night. She has a crush on my brother.

"I don't see you often," She says to him. Angela starts to laugh out loud. Gwen's flirting method won't work on my brother. If she thinks she's going to steal him from Angela there's no way. He's eight years older than Gwen.

"I'm Alex's brother," He says smoothly.

"Do you have, um, happen to have a girlfriend?" Gwen asks pressing her lips together.

"This is her," He presents Angela to Gwen who has a look of death in her eye.

"Whatever," She says moving on. "Your brother is a big jerk." She tells me. I hit her on the hand.

"He is not! He has a girlfriend and he's eight years older than you! Dream's over, move on, ruin another Christmas Eve, just not mine!" I shout at her and stomp off. I don't have time for her.

My mom announces that dinner is ready when I storm into the kitchen. She made a whole batch of peanut butter and anchovy sandwiches and made extra for my brother and Angela. I don't take one, leaving a ton for our special guests, the Biggley's.

I pick and choose at my dinner which isn't even soup. I'm pretty sure it's just chicken broth. There's no flavor whatsoever and it tastes disgusting.

"Yum!" Gwen beams from her seat with a peanut butter and anchovy sandwich in her hand. I laugh. I never thought that Gwen would like something that my mother baked, never mind a sandwich with anchovies on it!

"Here," My brother says handing Gwen his plate. "You can have mine, I think I'm full."

Gwen digs in to the next sandwich pushing aside her soup. I try to eat her mom's mashed potatoes, but they aren't good and they aren't mashed either. I don't think she cooked them, they just taste like hard potatoes in a mashed form.

"Alex, turn on that video you made," Dad demands. I sigh. I'm not looking forward to this. In the video I'm wearing sunglasses and a school uniform and singing in rap about how safety and education are important. Not fun.

The title menu appears on the screen. You can hear my voice in the background. I feel so stupid with everyone watching me. "Ed-u-cation," Junior edited it so it sounds all weird and cool. I watch as I start dancing and singing with my friends.

"I know, it's stupid," I say before anyone can.

"Ed-u-cation it's what has us learning," I close my eyes. Al and Angela start to dance while my mom and dad don't seem satisfied.

"Enough," My dad turns off the TV. "That was very, um, I suppose kind of nice of you to make," I take the video from him and wipe tears away. I just wanted to have a nice dinner with my brother and now I'm the laughing stock of my own house. "Uh, Alex I don't need the video that badly so you can keep it."

I start to cry harder. I guess my dad wanted me to make a music video that is boring and more educational than the one we had to make. He probably wanted Jazz or Classical music and us to be sitting down doing homework. I thought he wanted a fun, kid video that would want kids to enjoy school and keep safe. Obviously I had a different picture than he did, but being a Waters, that happens a lot in our house.

Al sets out a board game and Gwen runs to join him. I cry harder in my seat. I thought that Christmas was a fun time of year. I didn't think someone was going to steal my brother from me on Christmas Eve.

"Alex!" my brother calls. "Come play," I shake my head but join them anyway.

"You were so stupid in that video," Gwen whispers to me as I sit down.

"Whatever," I snap at her. She turns away and starts gushing about how much she loves Christmas Eve and board games are a tradition at her house and how she loves that my brother did a tradition and how they have so much in common.

My mom and dad are quietly listening to Mr. and Mrs. Biggley and Gwen's older sister, Julie. I try to hear what they're saying, but my parents don't say a word, they just politely listen to Mrs. Biggley and her outrageous comments on our Christmas decorations.

"I'm glad I'm home for Christmas, Alex," Al gives me a hug.

"I'm glad you are too," I smile.

Jackie

"Um, a cinnamon roll with chocolate chips and sprinkles!" Rosie orders off the menu. Midnight Sweets has become our 'the baseball club for girls' meeting place. My grandma made special reservations so that we can count our money and sign up our team.

"Who knew cinnamon rolls could get worse for you," laughs Caroline. It's true; Midnight Sweets has taken my favorite treats and added more sugar.

"Take it easy, Rosie." My grandma says. "You have to eat right to be when you're an athlete."

"Yeah," I add. "But Midnight Sweets as a weekly meeting spot ruins eating right."

The Baseball Club for Girls isn't spreading around town yet. Rosie keeps saying that the boys are just going to laugh in our faces because they know that they can beat us. Seriously, two practices hasn't helped our case and the dancing and parades don't help either. We don't have nearly as much baseball playing experience as we would like.

The Riverside Waters Athletic Association President has the choice to let us play or send us away. I'm hoping he notices that baseball isn't just a boy's sport and that girls can play too, that only is if we find out that we're good. Rosie still thinks there's such thing as fourth base.

I already know that I want to play 1st base. Alex wants to be a second base-chick (as we call it). I think Caroline is covering 3rd base or center field and Rosie wants to be a pitcher. You can't have a team with only four people, though. We need more.

"My dad can probably rent us some batting cages," says Caroline. "I think that the indoor ones are open during the winter, but I'm not positive."

"I want to practice pitching," speaks up Rosie. We turn and stare at her sadly. Rosie barely knows anything about baseball and she's doesn't have a baseball connection. Caroline, Alex, and I all do. Alex's brother plays professionally. Caroline's dad is a sports announcer and my grandma used to play during World War 2 and my grandpa played before World War 2.

Rosie thinks that home plate isn't a thing and that there isn't such thing as an ump. She says that's the second batter.

"Um, Rosie why don't you play a much simple position, such as shortstop," My grandma shoots

Rosie a shy smile. Rosie looks away for a second and then turns back.

"No," She snaps. "I want to be a pitcher."

"But Rosie," Alex butts in. "Being a pitcher is hard, you have to make sure to throw a curveball, a fastball, and other kinds."

"What?" Rosie beams. "Uh, Alex, newsflash there's only one ball."

"You need to see a baseball game." I tell her.

"Too bad it's, you know, January," says Alex.

I nod. I wish we had thought of this club sooner. Now we have to deal with stupid weather issues. Its way too cold to practice and the professionals are on break. I wish it wasn't below thirty degrees outside.

"Positions can be figured out later," Grandma announces.

"Why not now!?" Rosie questions.

"We don't have enough people right now," Grandma continues. "If you can actually find other players then we'll figure it out."

"Okay," Rosie sighs. I hope she doesn't ask the Pom team to join or anything. Alex told us about her Christmas Eve with Gwen Biggley and her family and it sounded terrible. Who knew that someone she was so mean? Back in elementary school, Gwen and I were super close; I mean elementary school was only a year ago so about a year ago. I didn't know she was so mean.

I hope that people who actually are dedicated and willing join our team. I don't want to lose each game. That would just prove that girls shouldn't play baseball and that's embarrassing.

***

I didn't think that I would ever have to visit the President's office. The president of the Athletic Association of Riverside Water's that is. I can't even imagine how much fun it will be playing on the baseball diamond in the sun. I'm so ready to play, that is if we get through the president.

"Hi," Caroline says politely setting down our clipboard with paperwork. "My name is Caroline, Caroline Taylor and I'm part of The Baseball Club," She starts to quiet down.

"Keep going," We encourage her.

"Actually, it's a baseball club, but just for girls because your athletic association doesn't say anything about girls playing baseball, or any sport for that matter." Caroline continues.

"Thank you, miss, but don't you know about our Pom squad and cheerleaders? I thought that helped a lot," The president turns around from his chair and says. Alex turns red and gasps. The president of the Riverside Waters Athletic Association is Mr. Waters?

"Dad!?"

"Alexandria!?"

"OMG, smiley face!" Rosie mocks. I look at Rosie disapprovingly; this isn't looking too good for anyone. I don't think that Mr. Waters, who hates that Al Waters is in baseball will like the fact that Alex wants to play as on all girl's team.

"Uh, this is awkward, why don't I call my, uh, our coach to pick us up and you can enjoy the rest of your day and my grandma can talk to you about this later on." I say kindly. "Rosie," I demand in a quiet voice. "Let me use your cell phone,"

We begin to walk out when Mr. Waters stops us. "Alexandria, why don't you come home with me?"

Alex does a double take and turns toward her dad. She can't look up and doesn't walk, she just stands there frozen.

"Just go, Alex." Rosie says sadly.

"Why did you call her that?" Her dad demands.

"Alex?" Rosie asks. "We call her that, and Ally sometimes."

"Mom calls me Alex dad," groans Alex. "It's okay, just a nickname. I'm positive it's not against the law. Let's just go, okay?" She walks away sadly. I take a look at Caroline and Rosie my brain tossing up ideas.

"What?" Caroline says in a nervous tone.

"He didn't say no!" I cry and run out of the building. Caroline and Rosie chase after me. I dial my grandma's number on Rosie's phone and she hurries to come pick us up. I explain my idea which involves a little mischief.

I think we just need to work hard and make sure that we don't run into anymore problems – such as the one we just had with Mr. Waters. We also need to reword what we say.

"You want us to beg?" questions Rosie.

"I think we need to maybe demand," says Caroline.

"Yes," Grandma nods. "Demanding is good, not too much, but yes, demanding." I nod my head too. I wish that Alex would have found out that her dad was the president of the athletic association, but I guess she had no idea. Her parents do so many things around the city, but not in a good way. They're like control freaks and super involved.

"I bet I can get some girls to sign up," Rosie says.

"That's a great idea, thank you, but first we need to sign up. So what exactly happened when you talked to him?" Grandma asks.

"Um, well I started by telling him about the club and then he told me about Pom and cheer squads and how that was the options for girls." Caroline explains. "Then he turned around and Alex saw him and screamed 'Dad' and he screamed 'Alexandria' and then took her away and was super mad."

"Okay, but he didn't say no?" asks my grandma.

"No," Caroline replies. "He was going to tell me about cheer and Pom I think."

"That's good then," my grandma says.

"When do we ask again?" I ask.

"Not yet, but we are going to be a team soon."

Alex

"I thought we made that clear that you were in dance," snaps my mother as she walks into my bedroom. I don't look at her. I wait for her to say more. "I didn't want you to dance because I knew you wouldn't stay committed,"

"I'm not quitting dance," I whisper. "I'm just joining this other club too for my friends and Al's sake. I'm not a quitter Mom," I've never quit anything, ever and I'm not going to start quitting now.

Since Dad met the baseball club for girls he's been pretty angry. I heard him on the phone with an athletic association sponsor who told him he was crazy for not providing the girls in the city with a sport. I thought the person on the phone was going to get fired that's how mad he was, but Dad just ended the conversation and had an 'emergency' meeting with his team.

My parents owning practically the city is a bit annoying. Whenever we are supposed to have a little of something, my parents make us have a surplus. Whenever we are supposed to have too much, my parents want to conserve and not make as much. They own everything too and the school board and the PTA services.

"Come on I don't want to be late," I have dance today and I'm missing our baseball practice. My mom and dad have been really good about getting me to dance now more than ever. I joined when I was little and my parents were worrying that I wasn't ever going to have a good job because I was in dance, but now because I want to play sports they are rushing me to dance and making sure I'm never late.

"Your dad won't explain this club to me," She snaps when we get in the car. "I want to know more,"

"I don't really know," I reply. "My friend Jackie pointed out that we couldn't practice or play baseball because there aren't any girl sports on Dad's signup list and menu. So we formed a club for girls who want to play baseball too, so that we could have a girl's team on the list."

"You didn't think about the fact that Dad has POM and cheer," Mom protests. I don't think that POM and cheer can be counted in the Riverside Waters Athletic Association because that's run by the Riverside Waters Schools, not the athletic association. "Dad has enough teams too, Alex, he probably doesn't have room and Al plays baseball too, you dance."

I'm not on board with my mom's idea and yes I dance, but can't I do something else like play baseball?

***

I tuck our permission slip in my binder and keep walking. Our field trip this year is to the zoo. I don't find that as fun as the other grade trips. Eighth grade gets D.C., seventh gets Chicago and the sixth graders are traveling down Riverside Avenue to the zoo!

I try to forget about the boring trip and walk down the halls instead. Jackson Spicer passes me and for a second I think he's going to ignore me when he stops me. My heart skips a beat.

"Hey Jackson," I smile. Jackson is on my dad's team and he's super nice. I stop in my tracks and stay still. "What's up?"

"Nothing much," He replies. "Hey, so your dad, my coach, had a meeting with us about your club."

"Yeah, it was stupid." I lie and start to feel guilty immediately. I love the baseball club for girls, I shouldn't say I don't, but it's Jackson Spicer!

"No, no, no, I thought that was super cool," He tells me.

"I love the club," I perk up and laugh, he laughs back at me. I start to feel stupid all of a sudden.

"You guys should come to a practice!" He suggests. I laugh.

"It's February!"

"You'd be surprised when we practice," He says.

"I am," I mumble. "Do you practice at Pine Tree Park?" I ask him. He nods. "We do too, well now we do, I hope my dad lets us play." Coach Ruth told us to find a couple more people and I was able to find some from dance and Rosie got some too.

"He will, I think so, I don't think he's afraid of you girls beating us," Jackson laughs. When I don't say anything, his laugh turns dark. "Not that you couldn't."

"Yeah," I whisper. Too bad we won't.

"Aren't you on cheer or something?" He asks me. I shake my head. Dance is probably what he's thinking, but I don't bother. I don't expect Jackson Spicer to remember what I do after school, but he was close enough to make me appreciate that he was trying. "See you in Math," he says and continues going, out of the corner of my eye I see him run into Caroline and start to chat her up – which is hard to do because she doesn't talk much – maybe he's trying to talk to all of us, I don't know why.

I barely make it to the lunchroom right before the lunch bell and struggle to find Rosie and Jackie sitting at a table that has two seats left. I sit down and unpack my lunch with an irritated Caroline coming up behind me.

"Jackson Spicer just talked to me," She says in an odd voice. She sounds slightly confused.

"Me too," Rosie says.

"Me," I add.

"He did to me too," Jackie nods.

"I wonder why," Caroline questions. "I don't think it has anything to do with me."

"Student Council," explains Rosie. "He's running for president and needs to be extra nice to everyone." She eyes him in line and talking to someone. "See,"

"Uh-oh," I comment in a sarcastic voice. I eye Gwen who is passing out buttons and cookies. Gwen can't ever run against Jackson. She's had a crush on Jackson since we were in diapers. I like him too, but not as much as she does.

"I know," Rosie continues. "Jackson and her are so going to date soon I can tell," I sigh. My chances with Jackson are over if that's the case. "She wants to be his vice president. Have you seen those cookies? The campaign name is 'JS-GB forever'."

"I want to run." Caroline squeaks.

"You should!" We all cry. She turns her head and smiles nervously. I want Caroline to beat Gwen out, but she could never win if she continues her shy streak. The Student Council president has to talk a lot.

"No, no."

"Come on." Jackie coaxes. "You're super kind to everyone,"

"You have the grades," Rosie adds.

165

"And you're a Taylor! Mrs. Adams and them love your sister!" I point out. Caroline hates that everyone is always thinking she's Cece and that she's being compared to her, but this time it could be an okay thing.

"I guess." Caroline mumbles.

"Louder," snaps Jackie.

"I GUESS!" Caroline screams. The whole lunchroom stares at her and laughs. She hides her head and is too embarrassed to turn back. "No, no, no, I can't run."

"Yes you can," Rosie says faithfully. "Your baseball club for girls is willing to do whatever and I mean whatever it takes to make you the student council president. You need to be committed, you need to work hard!"

Rosie says committed just like my mom said it the other day. That I need to be committed, I need to stay committed to dance. I am, but maybe I need to try harder, just like Caroline needs to try harder when it comes to her student council campaign. She wants to do this, but she is too shy even sign up.

"I will be the campaign manager." declares Rosie.

"You know she's not trying to be president of the U.S., right?" asks Jackie.

"Yeah, but with Jackson and Gwen running I don't think it would hurt to act like it is." Rosie rips out a piece of her notebook paper and hands it in to one of the lunch monitors. She starts drawing a big sign that says CTAYLOR FOR STUDENT COUNCIL PRES.

"I don't know," Caroline says. "I bet that Gwen and Jackson will get all the votes." We turn to see Gwen and Jackson who are being as nice and kind as possible to student body.

"Aw," I laugh. "They are so cute together,"

"Shut up," says Rosie eyeing Jackson, she likes him too.

***

Caroline hands me another brownie to pass out. Student Council campaigning can be uglier than I was thinking. Gwen and Jackson have out sold us, out baked out, and are going to out vote us I bet.

Caroline's brownies have done well, though she's given out so many so far, but a lot of those people promised Gwen and Jackson they'd vote for them. Jackson and Gwen have done a pretty good job

167

campaigning with coupons for stores and more. The one thing that is super irritating is that Gwen has the nerve to buy cookies from Midnight Sweets, Caroline's aunt and uncle's shop and sell them for her own campaign.

"You idiot!" Gwen screams. I spin around and look just as Gwen and Jackson are in the middle of the hall with frosting and buttons spilled all over Gwen. "This isn't cheap!" She screams pointing to her outfit.

"I'm so sorry, Gwen." Jackson says, trying to pull her up. She slaps his hands.

"No!" She yells. "You, go away!" She stands up and trips again on her heels.

"Relax," Jackson demands at her, screaming. The teachers don't do anything; they just look probably cheering for Jackson because Gwen is such a snob.

"Don't tell me what to do!" she screams. "I quit your campaign. I can win too!" She struts off tearing away a button from her shirt. Jackson looks at everyone with surprise and fear in his eyes.

"Vote for me, Caroline Taylor! Brownies, anyone?" Caroline screams. A group of kids run up

to us and tear brownies out of our hands and
promise our vote.

I nod towards Caroline. With a snotty Gwen on the
ballot there's no way that people will want to vote
for her so they'll vote for Jackson or us. That works
a whole lot better than a peppy Gwen who everyone
wants to vote for.

"OMG!" shouts Rosie running down the hall with
Jackie. "So, I just heard that Gwen got in a big fight
with Jackson and she was hitting him and crying
and she apparently is removed from the election!"

"No," I correct her. "Gwen tripped and was super
mad at Jackson so she quit and is running for
president."

"That means that Caroline has a better shot!"
Rosie says.

"But wait –," Jackie stops us. "Who's Caroline's
vice president?"

"I don't know," I say.

"I thought it was Rosie," Jackie wonders.

"I am the manager!" Rosie whines. "Vice Pres is
diff from a manager!"

"I don't want to be a vice president," I resign.

"Me neither," adds Jackie.

"I need a vice president!" Caroline whines.

"Okay," Rosie groans. "If I must save the day I'll do it, just make sure that we win!" We give her thumbs up. "TAYLOR FOR PRES, DAWKINS FOR VICE PRES!" She screams on the top of her lungs. "BROWNIES!"

"Vote Caroline and Rosie!" I yell.

"Don't delay vote Taylor and Dawkins today!" Jackie sings.

I smile. I want my friends to beat Gwen Biggley and maybe even Jackson Spicer. Rosie cheers and throws out brownies to everyone. She bosses Caroline around to go stand and make people promise to vote her. I hope that Rosie doesn't let all this power go to her head because that may happen with her in charge.

"Uh, no brownie if you mean no vote," Rosie sasses to someone.

"Wow," Gwen says walking down the hallway. "That's a bit harsh, Rosie, just for a gross brownie."

"Shut it, Gwen." Rosie snaps.

"Well, Sydney and I are going to win by so much you're going to cry."

What an amazing comeback that Gwen could come up with, this is not a student council election anymore as I can see, it's much, much more.

Caroline

"Are you sure I can't stay home Mom!?" I cry. I've begged, I've pleaded, I've cried, but I still have to go to the zoo today as the class trip that Mrs. Adams is making worth 5 percent of our Science grade.

I hate the zoo.

When I was five my parents took me and Cece to the zoo and when it was time to go feed the giraffes and when I put my hand out it threw up on me!

That's not all; when I was eight my parents took me to the zoo and when I was in the room with the butterflies I sat under a hornet's nest and was stung five times!

Last year when I went to the zoo we went to the lions. I was scared of what happened last time I came, but worse because when I spotted a lion he spotted me and ran down towards me. There was a gate, but still. I hate the zoo.

"No, sweetie you have to go. Five percent is a lot and besides I think that this is a wonderful chance for your friends to show you how fun the zoo is. I promise you, Caroline nothing bad will happen this time." My mother hugs me. "No throw up, no stings, no lions coming to get you."

I frown. She can't promise that because how does she know what's going to happen?

I try to hold back tears on the bus. I shouldn't be this upset about going on a field trip, but I've never been to the zoo without my parents and if something happens I want them to be there not Mrs. Adams or any other Science teacher.

I wipe my wet eyes and make my way off the bus. I play over my mom's words in my head. No throw up, no stings, and no lions coming to get you. She talked to me like I was two and I was afraid of being potty-trained. I just don't want to be attacked by an animal or puked on or stung.

"Good Morning, Caroline. How's the student council been going?" asks Mrs. Adams. I know I hate that she's making us go to the zoo, but Cece was right about how nice and fun Mrs. Adams is. She's been in on my presidential student council campaign and really wants me to win. Not because I'm Cece's sister, but for once because she thinks I deserve it.

"Um, okay. Good Morning, Mrs. Adams." I hand her my permission slip. I've waited all week to turn it in; I was hoping my mom would change her mind.

"Mrs. Adams!" Gwen cries. "Here, take a cupcake in honor of my student council campaign." She hands Mrs. Adams a pink frosted cupcake and with one glance at me she ups her act. She smiles and hands Mrs. Adams a button and poster too. The teachers get a say in the vote as well, but only the generosity column part.

"Why, thank you Gwen." Mrs. Adams puts the button in her pocket. "Now run to class, you wouldn't want to be late for the zoo!" Gwen has Ms. Doodly for Science and Mrs. Adams is her math teacher. 1st hour science classes are going today. So Ms. Doodly, Mrs. Adams, and Mr. Adams' first hours are going today.

Alex is in Ms. Doodly's first hour and Jackie is in Mr. Adam's first hour. Rosie has Mr. Adams sixth hour so she doesn't go until Wednesday when sixth hour goes. She's upset because wants us all to be together, but I could use a Rosie break for a while.

I didn't know Rosie wanted to be my vice president so badly, she could've just run for president herself. She's bossed me around every single day about how I need to hand out more goodies and make sure students know that I'm the right vote. I don't want to be too annoying though, I just want to run.

"Your mom called me," Mrs. Adams says after I snap out of my student council daydream. Mom and Mrs. Adams are best friends. That's how much Mrs. Adams loved Cece. She, Mr. Adams, Mom, and Dad sometimes hang out which is weird, but kind of cool at the same time.

"What did she say?" I ask in a quiet voice.

"She said that you weren't very fond of the zoo," Mrs. Adams replies. I nod. "Caroline, you have no idea how much I hate the zoo. I'm not an animal person. I have two dogs at home but who ever said that dogs should live in cages? I don't want you to be scared so I made sure that you can stay by your friends. I didn't want to make you sound babyish, which you aren't I totally understand, so everyone is going to hang out with friends for safety."

"Thanks," I mumble, but smile. At least my mom made sure that Mrs. Adams new my fear of the zoo.

"Everyone!" shouts Mrs. Adams. "Sit down, please." I sit down at my seat and wait for Mrs. Adams to dismiss us. "Line up and please be good,

Ms. Doodly wants to talk to you all on the bus and don't be rude!"

I race to get on the bus first so that way I don't end up on the back. The back is where everyone loves to sit, but I hate being one of the last ones off. Alex and Jackie sit beside me once they're on.

"Good morning, students, I'm Ms. Doodly, this is our first school trip. I know technically it's not a whole school trip because only our first hours are going." Ms. Doodly says. "I hope you know that you are missing your second hour today and that we have second hour plan so it's okay for us to do this now."

Gwen raises her hand.

"Yes, Genevieve?"

"Why do we have to go so early?" she asks.

"The zoo offered a later time, but I have other classes to teach and we have other days for them. It's too complicated, Gwen." Ms. Doodly answers. "Now, this zoo is amazing and they expect you to behave amazing. You will have fun, but I want you to remember that this is five percent of your grade. My first hour kids, you know that if you don't behave what will happen." Ms. Doodly eyes all her kids. Alex looks back at Ms. Doodly and nods.

"What will happen?" I whisper.

"Five-percent lower on our grade," Alex explains. She has Ms. Doodly, who is nice, but can be really mean.

I didn't think that the zoo was open in the middle of February, but last year our Winter Wonderland light show opened in September, so maybe everything opens early. I'd have to ask Alex; her parents do all of that.

The zoo's calendar says that they open in February, which in my opinion is a little too early because there isn't many people here. The zoo is clean and super nice (besides the animals, who I hate). When I was thrown up on, one of the workers let me borrow this costume they get to wear. When I was stung, they made sure I had these leopard print bandages. When I was attacked (almost) they gave me a free souvenir. So, I like the workers and the zoo place, but not the animals inside.

"Hi, I'm Lori Adams; we rented the zoo out for the next few days as a field trip in the morning." Mrs. Adams says at the entrance area.

"Mrs. Adams?" asks Gwen. "Can we call you Lori?"

"I don't see a Lori Adams," The front counter man replies.

Mrs. Adams ignores Gwen and looks back on Mr. Adams and Ms. Doodly. "Either Lori Adams, Margaret Doodly, or Sam Adams, other than that I don't know."

"I have Margaret Doodly's class," The man continues. "I also have Sam Adams for tomorrow and the next day and a Mary Winderson tomorrow."

Mrs. Winderson is an seventh and eighth grade science teacher, even though this is a sixth grade only trip. I don't know why Mrs. Winderson would be going.

"Mr. Adams!" Mrs. Adams calls to her husband. He reports to her side as she explains the situation.

"Why is Mary going?" asks Mr. Adams.

"I'm not sure, um, our names are right here," Mrs. Adams points to the computer screen.

"Oh, yeah, sorry." The man hands them the tickets. We are spilt up into groups. Mrs. Adams explains that we need to meet back at the entrance by eight twenty.

Cold and rainy outside, the zoo isn't very nice in the morning in the middle of February. I look around to see if any of the animals are out, I don't hear animal noises and the wet environment probably has them asleep.

Jackie and Alex don't say much, they just look around too. I feel bad I'm the reason they can't do have much fun this morning. I bet a student council president isn't scared of the zoo.

"Look at what Gwen's doing!" Alex points. Sure enough, Gwen is handing out cookies and buttons in the zoo. I spin around and want to dart for her table and ask her what's she's doing, but I'm so shy I can't even move from my position and ask my friends why she thinks this is okay.

"Free cookies shaped like animals – because I love animals. All you have to do is promise to vote for Gwen!" she shouts.

A bunch of people run to her, promising to vote her and taking cookies and walking about the zoo just talking to their friends. Alex and Jackie start to walk her way, so I follow suit, regretting it already.

I don't want to deal with drama, especially at the zoo.

"Oh hi," Gwen says in her baby voice. "I'm guessing you want some cookies, but I'm only handing these out to students who will vote for me."

Sydney stares at her looking very confused. "You said to hand out cookies to everyone."

"Uh, not them." snaps Gwen.

"But -,"

"Shut up, Sydney!" sasses Gwen, handing out a cookie and a cupcake to the next person approaching her.

I turn away in disgust. I don't want Gwen to win the student council president election. Alex taps my side and shoots me an angry look. "You do something." She snaps.

"What?" I whisper back. She shrugs.

"I want to shove that cupcake in Gwen's face." Jackie whispers sternly.

This gives me an idea, but I'm too shy to shove a cupcake in her face. Alex shoots me and Jackie both a smile.

"I can't do that," I whisper to her. "I'm too shy and too nice,"

Alex's eyes get big. She picks up a cupcake off the table and smiles. "Don't worry," She says. With Gwen talking to someone she takes a bright pink cupcake and slams it into Gwen's face. She shrieks so loud it sounds like she's dying and takes another one and throws right at Alex.

Jackie grabs her container of frosting and looks at Gwen angrily. "Sorry," She takes the butter knife and smears it on Gwen's mouth.

"You idiot!" Gwen screams and throws another treat at her. "I hate you all!"

Chaos breaks out and soon everyone is throwing something in Gwen's bag. She screams in terror.

I panic and climb onto the picnic table and cover my head. Kids try and throw things at me so I lean backwards and tumble off the table into the water fountain behind it. I'm covered in water and trying not to cry. Another thing to horrible things that happen when at the zoo.

I sit in the water fountain crying and drenched. Mrs. Adams, Mr. Adams, Ms. Doodly and a few workers stomp over to the scene. Only a few kids aren't throwing food and were actually looking at the animals. Mrs. Adams spots me and pulls me up.

"Are you okay?" She asks.

I shiver, too cold to answer.

"You know what; we need to get you a towel and hot chocolate asap," Mrs. Adams takes me over to one of the gift shops and asks to borrow a towel. She throws it around me and runs back to the scene.

"Who started this!?" Ms. Doodly beams. She stares at me especially. Everyone stares at Alex and Gwen. "Well, who?"

"I have to say, Ms. Doodly." Gwen speaks up. "We all participated in the food fight, but Alexandria Waters was the cause. She attacked me with one of my treats that I bought! I say detention is a very worthy punishment."

Alex frowns.

"Uh, um, Gwen started it too." I mumble. Ms. Doodly looks surprised to hear this.

"Oh yeah?" snaps Gwen. She glares. "Says the girl soaking wet from falling into a fountain!"

"Continue," Ms. Doodly says to me.

"Gwen wasn't being nice," I whisper.

"Shut up," Gwen whispers to my ear so no one can hear her but me. "Nobody will vote for a tattle tale." I shoot her a sad look and she nods. "Nobody,"

"Okay," Ms. Doodly sighs. "I don't know that anybody is going to admit to starting this food war so let's go and deal with punishments later."

Since it's only been like a half an hour Mrs. Adams has to call the buses to pick us up. Mr. Adams makes us promise to listen and behave, but Ms. Doodly thinks we should all go back now because we're acting more like animals then the animals themselves.

Alex doesn't talk the whole way back. I didn't see any teacher say anything to her, but she still seems mad. Jackie doesn't say a word either. I guess that when you're covered in brownie and cupcake frosting you don't want to talk to anyone.

I'm still soaking wet even after I had the towel on.

I really hate the zoo.

Rosie

I walk home from practice, shivering. I don't think we should have practice in the cold, but we have new girls on the team and need to teach them. Most of them don't know much about baseball, but that's why they're learning, but I still don't know much either. That's why we need more practice.

The wind blows my hair in my face making it hard to see. I reach home safely at last and meet my mom and dad and Sundae in my living room watching one of my mom's old movies. My mom has been trying to get my dad and me to watch her movies, even though some aren't in English.

My mom has been better about her stardom since staying with us. After the parade, she said sorry for not wanting me or thinking of me. "Rosie, I'm sorry." She said after the parade that day. "I'm proud of you too. I didn't have any sports for girls when I was your age."

Mom has acted more like a mom now too. She takes our dog, Sundae, for walks, she cooks and cleans and she shops. I'm glad that she's back I want her to stay, but I know that she has movies to film and that she has a career in Paris.

"Hey Rosie," Dad says, taking my coat. Mom turns the movie down. She waves to me as I set my things down. "What are you thinking for dinner? Pepper Pizza or my famous stir fry?"

I go to answer when my mom steps in, looking offended. She gasps at him.

"Pizza or Stir Fry?" She gasps. "My parents, whom you haven't seen in forever, are flying into town FROM PARIS, and you're making pizza?"

I look at my dad, opened mouthed. I haven't seen my mom's parents in a long time, but I know that people who are coming from Paris probably don't want pizza or even stir fry. My mom puts her hands on her hips and goes into diva mode, giving my dad a stare down until he answers her.

"I'm sorry honey; I must have forgotten that your parents were flying in." He says in the form of a question. My mom takes a moment to not say anything, silence fills the room. I want to say something. I want to stick up for my dad and say that I didn't even know that Grandma and Grandpa were coming, but then I want to stick up for my mom and say that my dad probably should've made reservations ahead of time.

"Um," Mom tries to say something, but doesn't. She presses her lips close together and sighs. "I'm trying super hard not to freak out, but my parents are expecting dinner, at a fancy restaurant, in twenty minutes."

"You should've reminded me!" Dad cries.

"No, no, no," Mom snaps. "I think that you should've remembered or made reservations." Mom struts around the room with her hands on her hips. My dad puts his hand on his head and starts to freak out. I want to remind them that we need to have dinner with them soon, but I figure it's not such a great time.

"Pizza Township is down the block," I suggest. I expect my mom to laugh because she hates the Pizza Township, but she doesn't, instead she sighs. "What about Julio's?"

"On a Friday night?" laughs my mom. Julio's is always busy on a weekend, but reservations are worse. I can only imagine trying to get a seat now, even if Julio's has the most amazing food in Riverside.

"You know what," My dad says, frustrated. "I'll call and make sure that we get a table, don't worry."

"No!" Mom shouts, taking the phone from him. "How are you even going to get a table now?" She stands up stiffly, knowing that she's right.

"You're Adelynn Simone; I think they'll get us a seat." My dad makes us reservations and I run upstairs and change into a much nicer outfit. I clean my dirty face from practice and make sure that I look nice. I go with my pink flower dress with a black cardigan and my fancy dress shoes.

I hurry down the stairs running out the door with my mom and my dad. Sundae barks at us as we shut the door. I head into the car and my dad drives away quicker than ever. We arrive at the restaurant in time. Mom sits down at out nice table and tries to make the arrangements nicer than they are. Grandma and Grandpa show up soon after.

"Adelynn, Victor, and Rosie." my grandpa shakes our hands and sits down. Grandma picks at her seat, waiting for Grandpa to pull out her seat, he does and she sighs.

"Riverside hasn't gotten much nicer," She complains. Paris must be amazing because Riverside very nice.

"How are you?" asks my dad.

"Fine," answers Grandma sharply.

"Okay," answers Grandpa the same.

"Would you like anything to drink?" asks the waiter.

"I would," Grandma replies in a snarky voice. "One chocolate strawberry water," I look through my menu to see that, but there isn't chocolate strawberry water on the menu.

"Ma'am, we don't have any chocolate strawberry water. We have plain water," The waiter answers. He waves to me shyly. I think for a second and then see Junior Lockwood, Jackie's foster brother. "Hey Rosie,"

"Hi Junior," I smile. "Uh, water for me."

"Okay,"

"What kind of place doesn't have chocolate strawberry water?" gasps my grandma.

"This place, ma'am," Junior answers.

"She wants chocolate strawberry water," My grandpa snaps.

"Sorry sir, we don't have any."

"Uh, they live in Paris and uh, think that everywhere has chocolate strawberry water, I guess." I tell Junior. He nods.

"I can try to get you some," He says.

"Thank you," My mom steps in. She looks over at my hopeless grandparents and sighs. With any luck Junior can put a strawberry on the top of the cup and add some chocolate syrup to the water. I wonder how that tastes.

Grandpa and Grandpa continue making small talk and stare disgusted at their meals. I dig into mine, which I don't usually do, I try to be polite and talk to my family member, but I love Julio's so much that I eat faster than anyone else.

When Junior comes back with the drinks my grandparents stare at them in utter disgust. They pick the strawberry off and throw it onto their plates. Junior pretty much got them some chocolate milk, but made it more watery.

"This is ridiculous," My grandmother complains. "I want flavored water, that's all. Chocolate Strawberry water."

"What is wrong with this place?" cries my grandfather. My mom hides her head, embarrassed.

189

I fake a shy smile at Junior, who is in no mood. I can't imagine being in his position. He could lose his job because of my family.

"Grandma, Grandpa, you can't base your whole vacation in Riverside, Michigan on this." I take their drinks and hand give them back to Junior, who giggles under his breath. "How about we focus on the positives of this? You're having dinner with your daughter and her husband." I don't mention myself, hoping they'll do that part.

"And you," my grandma says lightly.

"Thank you, Rosie." my grandpa says.

"That reminds me," my grandma continues. "I brought presents," We all awe over the cheesy presents that my grandparents bring. My grandpa gives my dad his hammer (his best hammer, Grandpa likes to build things) and my mom gets a super pretty wedding ring that used to belong to my great-grandma. I wait for mine, but all Grandma hands me is a box.

"What is this?" I ask. I shake the box, I try and rip the box open, but nothing happens. It's just a cardboard box.

"A box," Grandpa answers.

"I thought you might want it," my grandma explains. "Open it, Rosie." She demands. I pry it open to find a bracelet on the inside. Rosie Ann is engraved across in a shiny gold.

"Thank you," I say, thankful.

This is my good luck charm.

Spring Training

"Shine, don't worry about being the best, remember to just do your best and shine."

Alex

I sit down on the bench and listen to Miss Ruth's directions. Ariel and Talia aren't listening, though. They play Rock, Paper, Scissors until I get up and then Talia shoots me a blank look.

"What are you doing?" She asks. I shrug and walk towards Caroline, Jackie, and Rosie, annoyed. The new girls don't know how to do anything. Talia and Ariel come with me, trying not to look stupid.

"We already have a team," I inform them pointing to Jackie, Caroline, and Rosie plus some other new girls. The other group of new girls is across from us. The two of them stare completely confused.

"So do I stand here?" asks Talia. She starts to move around so that her shoes make noise on the ground. "OMG, this is so cool." She dances some more. I roll my eyes.

"You go over to that group," I direct her towards the others.

"Ok!" says Ariel.

Miss Ruth walks up to our group to see the 'problem' we're having. There isn't a problem, though. It's Talia and Ariel. I stand there, angry. We were supposed to start scrimmaging a few days ago, but they put us off then, too. We start games in over a week.

"I think that we'll have Ariel and Talia stay here and two of you can join them, that way Rosie, Caroline, Alex, and Jackie will be spread out." Miss Ruth says. Rosie and Jackie decide to go and I'm stuck with Talia and Ariel. I grunt.

"Why?" I ask.

"Because the newer girls need help," She says sharply. I groan, and direct them to the dugout.

"I'm so bored," Ariel whines. "I want to go home," She sits on the bench and squeals. "I saw a spider!" Talia starts to scream too and pretty soon everyone in the dugout is screaming besides Caroline and me. I sigh.

"Ariel, Talia, Shelia, you're in the outfield." I direct them. Shelia runs out, but Talia and Ariel remain lost discussing the spider. "I said outfield," I

194

say louder. They jump and run to first and second base.

"Whatever," Caroline says when I start to move. "They don't understand anything," She stands out there by shortstop. I wait for someone to say that practice is over and we can go home, but nobody speaks up.

The hour passes by slow, with me having to tell Ariel and Talia what every little thing means. I smile when Jackson and his brother pick me up, though. Jackson has been super nice and he loves our baseball club. I know that he knows he can beat us, but I think it's sweet that he tries to assure me that his team stinks.

I run inside and check my email to see when my brother is coming home again, but he hasn't responded to me and the last he said was that his spring training has been awesome. I can't wait to see him play, but I've got my own practices to worry about, especially the signing up part.

Since my dad revealed that he was the president of the Riverside Water athletic association we haven't tried to get registered. The problem with that is that if we don't sign up by next week we don't even get to play at all, which is a problem.

I'm hoping that next week we blow everyone away. Rosie's pitching our first game. Rosie's our best pitcher believe it or not. She's way better than Marianne, our other pitcher and super duper better than Ally who is our backup pitcher.

I get a text message on my phone. REGISTER NOW – Athletic Association with ms ruth come on! Rosie texts me when my phone beeps again. This time from Jackie. WHERE R U? I grab my coat and run downstairs and then head back up. I can't say that I want there to be girl's baseball when I'm sweaty and gross. I quickly change and put my hair up and fly back downstairs. I run out the door.

My parents work around the city day and night and most of the time come home around four to make dinner (we have dinner super early) and then they head out again. They know that I have dance and practice and sometimes I stay after school, so they know where I am.

"There you are!" Rosie throws a note card at me. "You're supposed to read this after me." I put the note card down on the table and nod.

"What is this?" I ask her.

"Oh," She laughs. "We're registering. Your dad isn't here! Thank goodness, but all we have to do is say what we want, not a big deal. Why weren't you here?"

"I didn't know we were doing this now," I explain.

"I told you five," Rosie says checking her phone. I thought it was three! I had no idea that two hours had passed. "I did, oh and I think we have some quitters," She whispers to me, since Miss Ruth is talking to the register people.

"Who?" I beam, hoping that Talia and Ariel are the ones quitting.

"Marianne has swim on our game days and Christina wants to quit because she's on POM now." Rosie explains. I sigh. I'm stuck with the girls who don't know how to do anything, still.

"Girls," Miss Ruth says shushing us.

"Sorry," Rosie and I say at the same time, laughing. I cross my fingers that our sign up works and that we can start playing. Rosie walks up to the front with Jackie and Caroline and sighs.

"You don't know how much fun this club is," Rosie nods at us. "I really want to play and I think that there should be more sports for girls."

I read my note card. "I think this would be so much fun," I nod in agreement to everyone else. I stick my note card in my pocket.

"Okay then," The secretary says handing us back forms. "You are now part of the Riverside Waters Athletic Association, all I need to do is inform Mr. Waters our president and then I can get you some uniforms and we'll be all set."

"Uh," Miss Ruth stares desperately at us to come up with something. I sigh. My dad is going to ruin my chances of having a sport other than POM or cheer in our town. This isn't fair. "This is actually Alex Waters, his daughter she already told him about this."

"Yeah," I nod. "His team is playing us next week!"

"Okay then," the lady hands us forms and papers. "Fill this out and then I'll order the uniforms when you hand this back into me. Thanks," Miss Ruth passes our uniform order form around. I fill out my size quickly and Miss Ruth hands in a picture of what our uniforms should look like.

I jump up and down with Jackie, Rosie, and Caroline once we're out of the building. I dance around and I feel my ankle turn weak. I sit down and recognize the same feeling when I fell off the pyramid in dance. "I can't walk home," I tell Miss Ruth. I see my dad walking out of the athletic center.

"Mr. Waters!" Miss Ruth calls to my dad. Dad turns around and walks towards me, my ankle still hurting. "Can you drive Alex home? I'm afraid her ankle is sore." My dad seems confused, but helps me off the wooden bench.

"Sure," he says.

"What do you think is wrong?" asks Jackie.

"I'm not sure," I answer.

"Let's go now," My dad pulls me away and puts me into the car without hurting my ankle. I wave to my friends as he drives us away. My ankle's not hurting too badly now. "Is your ankle okay?" He asks me.

"I think so," I reply. I rub my foot again. I haven't been to dance in a few weeks so how in the world could I hurt my foot there? At the same time, I do go to practice every day for baseball. I don't remember hurting my ankle.

"Hi," I say to my mom when I walk in, she waves. I go to ask for ice, but she's in front of the freezer and busy mixing everything into the soup she's cooking. "Um, I need some ice,"

"What did you do this time?" She moans. "Did you hurt your ankle again?" She hands me an ice pack and looks angrily at my ankle. "I don't see anything."

"It was hurting, that's all." I explain. She nods and continues cooking dinner. I head to my room and lay my ankle on my bed so I don't hurt it anymore that I already did. I make sure not to move my ankle for a long time. I want to play next week and with a sore ankle I don't know if I'll be able too.

Jackie

"Home plate!" My grandma sighs. "Rosie, if we want to play, you've got to learn. When was the last time you went to a baseball game?"

Embarrassed, Rosie hides her face and shrugs. She's embarrassed in front of the whole team. Not that they shouldn't be embarrassed too, most of them don't know what they're doing either.

"You have to work harder," I snap. I'm in no mood. Our game is in less than a week and half the team doesn't know how to play. Rosie ignores anyone who tries to help and she wants to pitch our first game? I get an idea. "Training!" I cry. "The boys have spring training, we should bring her to watch one of their scrimmages!"

Rosie throws my grandma an uncertain look. One that says 'no, please no, help me now'. It's too late, though. If Rosie doesn't know how to play, there's no way we can ever play.

"Let's go now," I suggest. Rosie hesitates and slowly makes her way towards me. The boys practice at Pine Tree Park all the time, which is where they are now. My favorite place to be during summer time.

Pine Tree Park is mostly amazing because of the name. Riverside Waters makes the malls, the stores, the everything about them. Mr. and Mrs. Waters name garbage trucks after themselves. Pine Tree Park is a perfect name for this park with the hundreds and thousands of pine trees surrounding you and animals everywhere. I'm surprised the Waters don't control this too, or else I bet some trees would die due to another shopping mall.

It wouldn't be a park in Riverside if it didn't include something new and big, which is why on the other side of the park you can see a field (or ten) for each sport. Big and bold with amazing dugouts and brand new sports equipment.

"Wow," Rosie ahs. Obviously this is her first time in a park, or this park, which is sad because this side shouldn't be considered a park with the brand new everything. I wish that sometimes everything wasn't so new.

I look around to find Mr. Waters and his team. I hope he doesn't remember us from that one day we begged to register. That would be a real nightmare.

"Jackie! Rosie!" some of the boys shout to us. Rosie blushes and gets lost on the new cheer deck because yes, they have that too. Rosie tries to stand on the deck and act out a cheer, I beg her to come down.

"Can we watch you guys?" I ask sweetly. They look over at Mr. Waters. He only knows Alex. I don't think he could ever remember Rosie, Caroline and I. That was a few months ago anyway. Besides, I used to try and watch them all the time last year.

"Oh hi, girls sure," Mr. Waters comes over and nods. He explains to us how it's simply just a scrimmage and no one really 'wins'. "You can be our cheerleaders," He says. Rosie beams at this and climbs on the cheer deck. I yank her down.

"Where's the ump?" asks Jackson Spicer curiously looking around. Sure enough, there isn't an ump in sight.

"Sorry, but the scrimmage is canceled," The other team's coach announces. "No ump, no game," Rosie frowns. She must have wanted to cheer on the boys really bad.

How stupid, I think to myself. Anyone can ump a baseball game – especially a scrimmage. I turn to Rosie, who is trying to find her way back onto the deck.

"Rosie can ump," I volunteer. Rosie jumps off the cheer deck and falls into the dirt. She gives me desperate, pleading eyes, but I make her go anyway. This could be good practice.

"No, no," She whispers, becoming shy.

Mr. Waters stomps over to us and stares her down. She squirms. "Do you know anything about baseball?" His eyes beam down on her like a lazor.

"I know that that right there is not fourth base," Rosie nervously points to home plate I sigh. I'm happy she knows that much – I don't know if she knows that it's home plate, though.

"That's good enough," Mr. Waters laughs. "Go stand behind home plate." Rosie stares at me again with confused eyes. I march over to Mr. Waters.

"Can I help?" I ask him.

"Sure,"

"Okay," I turn to Rosie. "We have to call if it's a strike or an out or a ball."

"How can we tell?" Rosie wonders.

"You'll see," I assure her and hand her a mask for protection. She tries not to touch the mask too much. She stares at it, terrified. She can't even put the mask on.

"Ew," She says. The mask is pretty dirty, but I make sure to wipe the dust off mine before putting it on. Rosie won't even touch hers. Mr. Water digs out a pink, also old and dusty mask, and hands her it. "No thank you," She refuses. "I don't need a mask."

A ball comes in our direction and nearly hits her. She squeals. "Um, on second thought, this mask is nice." She puts the mask on and looks away, trying not to get hit again.

"Ball," I say.

"WHAT!?" She cries. "That was so an out!" I laugh. Rosie doesn't quite understand any of baseball yet, but I suppose that's why I brought her here.

"Rosie," I call time on the game. The players huddle up in as I walk over to a shaking Rosie. She closes her eyes and begins to cry. She ignores me when I call her name. Mr. Waters stares at us, annoyed. "One moment, please," I say. He nods.

"I can't!" She cries. "I don't know why, but I can't, Jackie. I can't stand here and ump a stupid game. If I can't do that then I obviously won't be able to play!" She bursts into more tears and cries.

"Listen," I demand. She turns her cry into a light whine. The boys stare at us. I glare. She looks up. I remember how I snapped at her a couple minutes ago about how she needed to work harder. I don't want her to be this sad.

"I'm sorry," She whines. "You and Miss Ruth and Mr. Jim said that I needed to work harder and I didn't listen because I don't think I can." She hides her head. "I want to, Jackie. You don't know how badly I want to win next week, but I'm scared."

"Try again,"

She stands up and puts her mask back on. She smiles at Mr. Waters and asks for another chance. He nods at her. "Thanks," She says. She starts calling the game all by herself. I sit down after a while because she doesn't need my help.

My grandma picks us up after the scrimmage is over. Mr. Waters invites Rosie and I back again.

Rosie laughs when he says that we are welcome to come to their first game. I wonder if he knows that we are most certainly showing up for that.

"So, are you okay now, Rosie?" asks my grandma.

"I'm ready," She says.

***

I head up to my room after we drop Rosie off and find a package on my bed. I rip it open and nearly cry to see what's inside. My grandma ordered me a photo album a couple weeks ago, of my mom. It was done by one of these special photo album companies. My mom's name is engraved on the top. I smile.

I wish that my mom could see me playing next week. I wish my dad would come too, but he hasn't been back since around Christmas time. He said something about his job being better.

"Do you like the album?" asks Grandma. I nod. "I got you something else too," She says and hands me another box. I rip through the pink tissue paper and pull out a shirt and a pair of pants. My uniform!

I examine the gray sweatpants with Heaters in glitter letters down the side and Jackie written above it in cursive. The shirt is a hot pink with

Heaters across the back and a number and then our team name across the front.

"Thanks, Grandma," I say and take the uniform and hang it on the back of my door. She smiles at me.

"Ready?"

I nod.

Rosie

I can't stress out enough about our first ever game tomorrow. I'm so nervous I haven't been able to focus on anything. I had an English paper due and I had to finish it really fast last night because I was so focused on watching a game on TV. To make matters worse, my mom might not be able to come. Her flight back to Paris is tomorrow and she wants to come, she really does, but they expect her back on her movie set.

She said that she would much rather come to our game then return to the set of her movie. I understand, though. She has a job that she has to report too.

I'm extremely nervous for the game, though. I don't know why I ever let them talk me into pitching the very first game. I don't want to now, the pressure is on and I'm so scared.

"Rosie," my mom calls downstairs. "Don't be late!" I run downstairs with my backpack in arm running. In addition to being nervous, I misplaced my lucky bracelet that my grandparents gave to me. I hurry into the car and run into school once we arrive.

"Hey Rosie," says Junior Lockwood. I smile. I'm in a rush and my locker won't open. My backpack falls down and Junior grabs it, I fall too. "You okay?" He asks. I nod.

"I'm still a little sleepy," I say shyly. I'm not in a good mood; I have two minutes to go across the school.

He takes my books and walks me halfway down. His class is by mine, but not exactly. He makes sure I'm get there without falling again. "You're up against the Dolphins tomorrow, aren't you?" He wonders. I nod. "I heard you're pitching," I nod again. "Okay," He says bye and walks to his first class. I regret not saying much, but I don't want to be reminded of the game tomorrow, I'm nervous enough as it is.

The student council results come in too today and I don't want to know the answer to that. I'm not surprised when I hear Jackson's name over the speaker and cheering from most of the people in the classroom.

"Nice try, Rosie." Jackson shakes my hand. I was kind of running for president after the whole zoo trip thing. They disqualified Gwen and Caroline for being involved in the food fight at the zoo. Sydney ran for president then and so did I. I lost, though, which is okay I didn't want to win anyway.

I want to win tomorrow, though and am determined to. After school, I head into my dad's office to ask if I can type my homework on his computer, instead his room is empty and the lights are all off. I don't usually hang out in his office because he has a lot of marketing and sales things in there and I might accidentally touch something I'm not supposed to. I'm drawn to something, though.

A poster on his wall has a baseball player on it, but not any old player, the person reminds me of him. He has curly dark hair and bright blue eyes. He's jumping up in the air and the picture almost comes to life.

"Rosie!" A voice calls. I quickly shut the door and hide behind a cabinet. He calls again and I start to hear someone opening the door. I crawl into the cabinet again, insuring that I'm not seen. My dad turns on his computer and his screensaver is the same as the picture on the wall.

I slide on a piece of paper below my feet. I pick it up and open it. 'Dawkins Quits'. I gasp.

My dad played baseball.

I bang my head and BOOM! A basket tumbles off the cabinet. My dad flings around sees me trying to come up, I bang my head again. "Ouch," I whine.

"Rosie Ann Dawkins!" My dad cries. "What on Earth are you doing?" I smile sheepishly and slowly creep out of from behind the cabinet.

"Sorry," I say, crawling out. I tuck the paper into my pocket, making sure not to drop it. My dad sees the paper, though and takes it from me in a second.

"What are you doing with this?" He snaps.

"I was looking!" I sigh. "Did you play baseball?"

"Yes," He says.

"Why didn't you say anything?"

"Because!" He cries. "I had to quit so your mom could go to Paris and be a movie star!" My dad gave up his dream so my mom could go to Paris.

"Oh," I whisper.

"I'm sorry, Rosie," He sighs. "I didn't think it was that important," I try not to laugh. I've been playing baseball for months and he could've helped! "Sorry," He says again.

"That's okay,"

I walk back downstairs to find my mom packing up her things. When she looks at my expression she laughs. "Did you find his secret stash of Victor Dawkins posters and news articles?" I'm in no mood.

"Kind of," I mumble. "How did you know?"

"Well," She sighs. "Your first game is tomorrow and I knew he wanted to say something and help you out, but he promised me that he wouldn't touch any of that stuff ever again," She takes out a photo album. "I wish I hadn't told him that I was more important, that I needed this job."

"What?" I ask, confused.

"I thought that him playing and me acting and you were there too," She combines into a big, long sentence that I don't understand. "Good luck tomorrow, Rosie. I know that you will be amazing, shine." She zips up her suitcase and puts it by the door. "Don't worry about being the best; remember to just do your best."

"Thank you," I hug her. I wish she was coming to the game. My dad has to work and I'm catching a ride with the Taylor's. It's okay, but I wish one of my family members were coming.

The Taylor's minivan is already cooped up with a bunch of kids. Cece is sitting in the front with Mrs. Taylor, Cody and Ashley make up the back. Caroline and Alex are sitting in the seats behind Cece and her mom. I'm stuck in between Cody and Ashley.

Caroline's dad took the week off to see the game and has to go across the country afterwards to announce a game. My mom has to go across the ocean and she couldn't wait one more day. I sigh. I wish she or my dad were here right now. I wish I had on my lucky bracelet too.

Alex's dad doesn't know that we're on our way to play his team. He's in for a rude awakening, but it could be fun for us. I start to feel sick to my stomach. I don't want to ruin this game for my friends. I want to win so badly.

Coach Ruth and the rest of the girls are in the dugout when we arrive. I change from my nice dress shoes and put on pink cleats that my mom bought us. She said we had to match and had one of her designers design us all pairs.

My uniform is the best, though. I don't know how Coach Ruth got us these. They're amazing. I almost don't want to get mine dirty.

Riverside hires announcers to announce all of the games for them so it's like a real major league game. The announcers announce that we only have a couple minutes to prepare. I put on my hat that's pink and has my initials, RD, on top.

"Ready?" asks Miss Ruth handing me the ball. I shake my head. I don't think I can do this. I'm too afraid. My hands are shaking, I have butterflies in my stomach and I can't see a thing. I'm scared.

The other girls call me over for a little cheer. I mumble the words barley and don't put my hand in that much. My enthusiasm isn't here; I'm not ready to go.

"Rosie," Miss Ruth sees me freaking out on the bench. "It's okay; I promise you'll do fine. You're nervous, that's very normal." Mr. Jim comes over and pats my back.

"Don't worry," He says.

I nod and make my way to the very front of the dugout, trying not to freak out again. My friends join me, probably not worried at all. One by one we walk out of the dugout onto the field. The boys don't laugh or say anything. They stare and turn to Mr. Waters, who looks surprised. Jackson Spicer is probably the only boy who knew that we are playing them too, the rest had no idea.

"Ha!" yells Justin Winderson. "Girls, the girls are playing us? This will be easy." I hide my face at the mound and sigh. This isn't fun so far and I haven't even pitched or anything yet. I'm more nervous than I was.

"Rosie Dawkins?" I hear one of them laugh. I spin around and shoot a glare at someone; I don't know who said that.

I try and throw the ball aimlessly. I have a few practice pitches I can throw. Our catcher, Alyssa, mouths the word 'no' when I throw so off that I nearly hit the ump in the face. And the ump is really tall.

The boys howl with laughter when I miss again and I feel like giving up. I have nothing left in me, nobody's cheering me on. I want to quit. Alyssa comes up to me looking irritated. She isn't the nicest and probably is angry with me because I'm already upset.

"What is up!?" She snaps. She takes off her mask and stares at me, her eyes angry.

"I'm scared," I manage to mumble.

"Don't be!" She storms back off to behind the plate. She shoots me evil eyes and demands me to throw. I throw, this time missing again, but not as badly. The boys laugh again and the ump wants one of them to come bat. I sigh.

"Rosie!" calls a voice. I turn around. Alex, Jackie, and Caroline wave to me and smile. "You can do it!"

I throw at Justin Winderson who jumps out of the way. "I think she was trying to hit me!" He whines in a lying voice. I shake my head and shoot him a glare. I did not.

I throw and I throw and I throw. And time after time I miss and he jumps out of the way. He slowly walks over to the base after I throw the fourth ball when the ump calls him back. "STRIKE," The ump calls louder. I stare back at Alyssa who looks unpleased and instead turn back to my friends who jump up and down with happiness.

Justin calls out Mr. Waters to tell the ump he's wrong, but Mr. Waters has no say says the ump and that Justin needs to suck it up and try again. I smile.

But smiles only last so long because I end up walking him anyway. Miss Ruth and Mr. Jim try hard not to look at me and instead focus on Jackie and Ariel who need to make sure Justin doesn't try to steal.

"Um, steal what?" asks Ariel, dumfounded. The boys laugh. Oh whatever, this couldn't be more embarrassing than it already is.

Oh, but I'm wrong.

When it's our turn to bat, we strike out and strike out. And most of it is because we have Ariel, Talia, and Marianne at the front of the lineup. They seriously swing and miss at each pitch. "Oops," Talia says coming back in.

I don't do much better as the game goes on and Ally our backup pitcher has to come in. We end up with two hits and a few base runners because Caroline walks and so does Alyssa.

We end up losing one to ten. I try not to cry once it's over, but I don't know what to do. I can't believe that we lost by that much. That's awful!

Miss Ruth and Mr. Jim assure me that I did my best and that it wasn't my fault. Alyssa, Ally, and Marianne decide to gang up on me, though and say that I shouldn't have pitched so horribly.

"I got you out of that," Ally informs me.

I choke up grabbing my things and heading out to Caroline's car. Jackie, Caroline, and Alex haven't said anything to me since the game ended. I try not to be upset by this.

"Wonderful job, sweetheart," a familiar voice says. I turn around and beam at my mom and dad standing behind me with flowers. I burst into tears.

"What's wrong?" asks my mom.

"I'm so glad to see you!" I hug her.

"What about me?" asks my dad.

I hug him too. "Wait," I stare up at them. "Don't you have to work and you should be in Paris!" My parents both nod and I start to feel awful. They should be in Paris and at work and instead they watched me fail. I cry again.

"Hey!" My mom says sternly. "Rosie Ann Dawkins you stop that crying this instant!"

"What is the matter?" asks my dad. "Aren't you glad we came?"

"No!" I shout in tears. "You shouldn't have come! I did awful! I didn't do anything right and w-why are you h-here?"

"Well," My dad says. "I told the store I wanted the day off to see you!"

"And I wanted to see the game and the directors said I could come in a day late," explains my mom.

"You did the opposite of fail!" My dad says. "You tried,"

I don't say anything back. My parents tried to be supportive, but I'm not in the mood. I wish that they didn't have to see me fail. I wanted to win so badly. I thought we were going to win. I had practiced so much and didn't win.

"It's okay," My mom says.

"Don't worry," My dad adds. I still don't reply.

My phone vibrates in my pocket and I look to have a bunch of new messages. A bunch of girls from the team texted me. SORRY some say from Ally, Ariel, and Marianne, the ones who were mean to me about losing. I don't text back.

I get another text. NEXT GAME DAY –
THURSDAY

How great.

Caroline

The crowd roars and I'm the reason for their happiness. Everyone is screaming and cheering my name. I hold a trophy in my hand. I'm the winner. I won. I'm a hero to the mathletes junior honor club, but it's all just a dream.

"Caroline!" shouts my mother, shaking me like crazy. I'm in a deep sleep and I don't wake up. Instead I fall back into sleep. My mom shakes me once more. This time nearly knocking me off my bed. "CAROLINE!" She screams. I wake up.

"Good morning," I say in a sleepy voice. She laughs. I'm super tired and that dream made me want to stay in bed all day. My mom shakes me again forcing me up. I stand up and groan. I don't want to go to school, not after the awful game last night. I'd rather be asleep, dreaming that everyone is looking up to me. My dream was about the Mathletes Junior Honor Club, which I'm not even sure I qualify for, but still. I won something in that dream which is way better than the game last night.

The boys took turns teasing us after the game and asking why we bothered to show up. I was hurt and didn't talk to anyone, like I do when I'm upset, on the ride home. I was embarrassed that we didn't try. We're better than that and I for one thought that we could've won.

I didn't assign blame to any certain person because I think that we all need some improvement. Ally, Ariel, and Marianne decided to attack Rosie because she didn't pitch her best, but they didn't do anything either.

Rosie announced to Jackie, Alex, and I that she wasn't going to our next game. Miss Ruth says that she has to, but Rosie probably won't show up anyway. It's not like this is important to her. She still has POM and cheer and that stuff. The rest of us really want to win this one, though. I know we can.

I grab my glasses and stare at the clock. I do this every morning to see how much time I have, but this time the clock reads six fifty, which is ten minutes before I leave. I run out my bedroom door. Ashley and Cody aren't awake yet and Mom and Dad are busy sitting at the table reading the newspaper.

"UH!" I shout. Cece is nowhere in sight, probably at school. My parents stare at me and laugh. This isn't funny! "I have to go!" I cry.

"I know," my dad says without any emotion. I stare at him with my eyes wide open. I need to go now! "I thought you might want to skip,"

"SKIP?" I ask. I've never missed a day of school in my life; either have any of my siblings. "Where's Cece?"

"At school,"

Obviously, she wouldn't miss school if she was deadly contagious.

"Mommy!" cries Ashley coming out of her room. She rubs her eyes and puts her small glasses on. "Caroline woke me up! Why aren't you at school?"

"Because," My mom says, grabbing her coat. She laughs at me. I look at the time. Eight minutes. "Do you want to go to school?"

"Yes!" I shout. I had a viral throat infection in third grade and couldn't talk and I went to school to keep my perfect attendance. "Why did you wake me up if you didn't want me to come to school?"

"Because your dad has a flight," Mom reminds me. My dad is flying across the country today to go back to his job. I had so much fun with him I forgot that he was flying back. "Do you want to come with me?" She asks.

I nod, but I've never missed school.

"Too bad," My dad says shaking his head. "You can't."

"Yeah sorry," My mom says. "You better get ready for school you have about five minutes before the bus."

"Why can't I?" I ask.

"Because I'm not going back," He smiles. I burst into tears. My dad is staying! "I quit that job; I didn't like being away forever and ever. The station hired me to work as a video reporter and assistant news writer for their website. I took the job,"

"Does that mean no more leaving!?"

"I have to leave sometimes to gather information and meet with players, but not a lot." He replies.

"Hurry up," My mom says. I run to my room and get dressed quickly. I run out with my backpack and bunny slippers on. My mom and dad laugh at me. "I'll drive you," My mom says and relived I change shoes and sit down. I have more time to get ready now. I smile at my dad and hug him tight. I'm so happy that he's staying.

But the happiness doesn't last long.

225

All anyone can talk about at school is how we played and lost our first game last night. Some of the girls on our team try to say that they quit and that it wasn't their fault.

"Yeah, you know that annoying girl, Rosie Dawkins?" Ally Beaker says to Sydney Mister and Gwen Biggley. "She ruined it for us, she can't pitch."

"She tried," I defend.

"What are you doing?" Gwen snaps, glaring at me with her dark blue evil eyes.

"UG!" shouts Ally. She turns to me. "You were awful too,"

"Why don't you quit then!" I say loudly, my anger attacking me. "If you're going to blame everything on the rest of us then why don't you quit?!"

"Shut up," Her voice is demanding and icy cold. The three of them put their hands on their hips and flip back their hair. Gwen's population is increasing and my friends, kind of friends, are being sucked into it. Ally, Sydney, and Gwen head off to Talia and Marianne who start to nod and laugh and I'm afraid that our club is going to collapse when everyone quits.

That is if everyone quits. I hope that they don't.

**

"Caroline hurry up!" my mom shouts into my bedroom. I want to make sure that this game is perfect and so much better than our first. I grab my bag and my shoes and run out the door. This needs to be perfect and I'm going to try much harder than I did last time.

I'm nearly late to the game because we have to drop Cece off at the high school for one of her projects. "Oh, good," Miss Ruth says when I walk in. "I thought you weren't coming," For some reason she seems oddly relived. She acts like I'm the only one here. I squint my eyes, because I had to take off my glasses, and stare at the field. Most of us are here, but I notice that Ally, Alyssa, and Marianne are yet to show up.

Jackie, Alex, and Rosie come up to me frowning. "Ready to fail?" asks Rosie in an annoying voice. "I heard the other team is already making bets that we're going to lose,"

"Oh whatever," sighs Jackie. "I want to win and they don't know we'll lose!"

"I heard they want us to join the bet," Alex adds.

"Maybe we won't lose," I say softly.

"Yeah right," Rosie laughs turns sour. "I would squeal and throw myself headfirst into that mud if we won,"

"Okay," I turn to her and walk to the mud. This park is famous for the mud puddles and someone as clean as Rosie would probably never touch that mud. The mud stains things too, once I slipped and my favorite shirt was ruined. "I want you to if we win,"

"Whatever, Caroline," She snaps and irritably walks back into the dugout.

I sigh. I wanted to make them all laugh so that if we do lose it won't be so bad. I know that now with them irritated and I'm a cranky now too we can never bring ourselves together to win.

Once we start I head out to the field and smile at the audience that came to watch in our fancy bleachers. I feel like I'm a real player when I'm playing here. My mom and dad give me thumbs up and wave their sign for me. 'Go Caroline, Go!' it says.

Rosie is pitching today's game because she says that she wants to redeem herself from last game and the pitching disaster. She throws and misses by a lot, but not quite as bad as last time. Alex runs to the back of the fence to pick it up. Since Alyssa, Ally, and Marianne still haven't showed up, Alex is filling in as catcher. "Sorry!" Rosie shouts. Everyone in the field takes a long, deep sigh.

Rosie doesn't do better with her practice pitches, but the ump demands that we start and before we know it the bases are loaded from three walks. This team doesn't even try to hit, they wait patiently until the ump says ball four.

After a while the ump says that this inning has gone on too long and that we spent way too much time on this one inning. My legs start to feel weak because I've been standing forever and I want to sit down. Once we're in the dugout, Rosie sits down on the bench hides her face in her hands and begins to cry.

The rest of the team doesn't say anything either and Miss Ruth comes back into the dugout after having a discussion with Mr. Jim, the ump, and the other coach. "We lost," She announces. This isn't much of a surprise, but is a disappointment.

"Uh, the game isn't over," Jackie points out. We barley played at all, but that's because the boys kept us on the field.

"Our game time is up and that was a mercy." Miss Ruth says. I look at her and everyone else puzzled. "That means that they had over twenty points and we had none."

"So we have to stop?" asks Alex.

"There's no possible way that we can catch up,"

I want to cry, but I'm not going to throw a fit because we lost. Even if we lost again and this was worse. Rosie starts to pick her head up and stops crying, but when she hears the game's over she bursts into tears again.

"I knew we wouldn't win," She's sour and aggravated. I snap.

"See!" I point my fingers at her. "If you would have a positive attitude then maybe we would have had a chance! A chance! Do you know the giant difference between what happened and a chance?" My usually quiet voice starts to become loud and powerful. The team stares at me. "Um, I'm sorry." I whisper and sit down.

Nobody says anything and Rosie grabs her stuff and scowls at me when she leaves. My stomach growls and I can already tell that this game is going to being the whole team down.

The Baseball Season

"This is our best game ever."

Alex

"I'm not sure," I reply shaking my head a little bit and looking into the crowded hallway absolutely flooded with kids. I almost trip and fall, but catch myself and turn back to Jackson. He waits anxiously. Jackson wants The Baseball Club for Girls to be over. He says that we're competition and nobody wants two teams in Riverside anyway. I disagree, but since its Jackson we're talking about I at least take it into consideration. He's been the nicest to me and I think that he likes me too! Which would be SO amazing and a miracle since I've had a crush on him since practically forever.

I just hope he's not using me to some advantage. I'm pretty sure that he wouldn't do that, but you can never be sure. I don't think he would do that, though and that's what I truly think too, not because he's Jackson Spicer.

"Come on," He coaxes. When we lost yesterday, he was in the bleachers watching us. He said that we don't have that much energy. I explained how Caroline desperately tried to pump us up, but nobody wanted to hear it, Rosie wanted nothing to do with it. She was so miserable and won't speak to any of us. I think she wants to quit.

"I said I'm not sure!" I repeat, but laugh. I don't know what to do. I kind of have outgrown dance, I missed our last recital and I haven't come to many practices, but I still think dance is my passion. I don't want to give up the baseball club, though. I think that we need a little work as Caroline might say. Or we need to TRY as Jackie might quote. Rosie's quote would be 'shop, shop, diddly do I'm a POM girl and a baseball player too!' I adore my friends.

Jackson turns the corner and winks. "Think about it," I nod and feel special until Gwen starts chatting him up. She looks nervously towards me and I smirk. She turns back to him.

I know not to even try to bring up quitting to Jackie; I know she'd kill me. She misses her mom, who passed away, and her dad, who is somewhere across the country working in business. The club is her favorite activity after school and I know that she would really hate to quit.

I don't want to say that I want to quit to Rosie either. Not only is she not speaking to us, but she doesn't want anyone to dare to bring up losing the other night to her. She talks to her other friends and other people, but she wouldn't talk to us. I don't understand.

I spot Caroline walking down the hall and stop. I bet that Caroline would listen. I bet that she would want to quit too! "Oh, hi Alex," She says.

"I think that we should quit our baseball club!?" I say.

"Hello to you too," Caroline laughs nervously. "Umm, why?" I explain why this might be a good thing. She stands there listening to every word I say until I'm done. "No," She snaps, slams her locker, and leaves me stranded in the hallway.

"Uh, don't want away like that!"I shout to her. She hesitates and then spins around and in an angry fashion she waits for me to talk. "I think that this would be better and maybe we can help out the boys by being cheerleaders!"

She shakes her head vigorously. "Um, says Alex Waters who wanted to make a difference just like I did, just like Jackie and Rosie did! We all wanted this and here you are – the girl who HATES quitters, telling me to quit." She turns away and spins back. "You are so contradicting yourself and you know it!"

She marches off. I feel like I've been slapped. I thought that maybe she would understand and now I don't know what to think. I have a strong, strong,

STRONG feeling that The Baseball Club for Girls is about to get ugly and break apart fast.

**

I sit alone at lunch to give Caroline some space. I don't want to go sit with Jackie, Rosie, and Caroline who will kick me out anyway. I'm actually not sitting alone because of that. I'm by myself because they 'forgot' to save me a seat. As if. I know that they're mad at me.

Jackson saves me from loserville and sits down next to me with his friends, John Anderson and Justin Winderson. They start to talk about something totally boring and I wish I was sitting next to my real friends who would start a silly conversation and then fight over it and then end up laughing and Jackie spitting milk out her nose and Rosie nearly throwing up because she's spitting it up. Caroline would rush to grab some napkins and would start to laugh and control Rosie so that she doesn't start to get sick. I love and miss my friends.

"Did you talk to them?" asks Jackson. I nod and start to tear up. The procedure is already going down as I can see over his shoulders. I sigh. "So,"

I forget I'm talking to Jackson and I go to get up. He pulls my arm down and looks at me. "SO!" He says louder.

"Oh, uh I don't want to talk about it," I mumble. What did he ask me about again? I can't remember.

"Oh okay," He says. I turn away and walk towards my friends. I'm going to at least try and fix this problem! I don't want this to get any worse.

Jackie, Rosie, and Caroline are busy cleaning up the mess they made on the table. Jackie looks at me in disgust as does Caroline and Rosie. I'm even surprised that Rosie is even speaking to them, but with this on our hands I know she won't speak to me.

"What do you want?" Rosie snaps. She twists her neck and puts her legs on two chairs. "You can't sit here, quitter."

"Shut up!" I cry. "I'm not a quitter!" I feel punched in the face.

"Yes you are," Jackie corrects me. "Don't worry, Caroline managed to tell us all about how you want us to quit, yeah not gonna happen, sorry."

"Yes gonna happen!" I fly off the handle. My patience is done I'm done with them. I just want

237

what's best for our team and Jackson. I don't care much about friendship anymore even if I did a few minutes ago. I'm not going to stand here and take punches.

"Alex please go," Caroline whispers.

"Why?" I ask angrily.

"Because," She says.

"WHY?"

"Because I don't understand what happened!" She bursts into tears. "I thought that you wanted this so badly! I don't know what changed your mind, but whatever did, I'm sure it wasn't worth your friends!" She stomps away.

"Alex!" Jackson calls running up to me. If things couldn't get worse, Jackson just made them worse. "Did you guys quit?"

"Oh we quit alright," Jackie assures him. She walks away with Rosie and Caroline and bumps into me. "I hope your boyfriend was worth the pain, Alex." Then she stops. "Wait, I'm not your friend, *Alexandria*."

"What was that about?" asks Jackson.

I run off in tears.

This is over.

Jackie

I slam my door shut and run to my bed, in tears. I cry and cry and cry until I spot Jamal and Rak under my bed. I'm so cranky I scream at them. "GET OUT NOW!" They run out and start to yell for my grandma and grandpa to help them. I'm not in the mood.

Alex announced today that she was out of the baseball club for girls. I know exactly what happened. Jackson, her crush, probably found a way to crawl inside her head and make her do anything for him. Then he tricked Alex into quitting and she wanted to just like that because it was Jackson and she would do anything, anything for Jackson Spicer. What about friends? I keep thinking to myself. I thought best friends came before boyfriends. I guess not in her book. I kind of have a crush on Jackson too, but I would go to Rosie, Caroline, and Alex to tell them something before him. I know I would.

Alex is too in his trap to notice what he did to her and how big of a trick this is. He wants his team to win and doesn't really think that we're competition and that we can beat him. He wants Alex to think does, though.

I'm so upset that I don't realize how much time has passed and that it's nearly dinner time by the time I'm finished doing my homework and crying harder about our club. My grandma is the only one who can actually say if we are quitting, but I don't feel like explaining the drama to her or anyone for that matter.

"Hey," there's a knock on my door. Rosie and Caroline come in and sit on my bed and chairs. I don't look at them. My face is red and teary from crying. When I do look at them I don't feel so bad. Their faces are red too.

"So," Rosie says, trying to break the silence. Nobody is quite in the mood to say anything, though. I don't understand how one day you think you have friends and the same day they go against you. It's so stupid. I wish that she never would have thought about quitting. I would have said 'sorry I signed up for this and I'm going to do it,'.

"What do we do?" I ask them. Caroline shrugs and Rosie doesn't answer. I stare blankly into space. I don't know either. After lunch, Alyssa, Ally, and Marianne said that they heard that Alex was quitting and that the club was over so they handed in a note saying that they were quitting too. More girls did too, so we're pretty much down to the three of us.

Plus possibly Ariel and Talia, the two most useless girls on the team.

"I guess we quit," Caroline suggests stifling tears. I don't want to quit, though! I want to prove to everyone that quit that we didn't give up, but that's pretty much out of the question now. We have five girls. That isn't enough!

"I don't think so," Rosie says. "We need to try. Remember? We can't give up and winning isn't about if we win or lose. We need to TRY!" I agree with her by nodding. I mean we do have to try, but I think we need to try harder!

"What are we supposed to do, then?" I ask, puzzled.

"I don't know," Caroline mumbles.

We have some work to do.

***

Practice is pretty boring when nobody shows up. Grandma still has no idea that Alex and pretty much everyone else resigned and that we are done for. I know that Caroline, Rosie, and I can come up with something to make this work without giving up. We need some more time to think, that's all.

"Come on," Grandma shouts to everyone, well Rosie, Caroline, Talia, Ariel and I. "Where is everyone today?" She asks. Nobody answers. Ariel goes to start blabbing on and on about how everyone quit, but Alex for some reason walks in on time with a paper.

"Uh, I'm not going to be able to play because my ankle hurts," Alex says. I, along with Rosie and Caroline, snort. I'm so annoyed that she would come back here and quit by lying about her ankle. My grandma nods and looks over her paper.

"Really, Alex?" She questions her. "A broken ankle? I don't think so." Alex shrugs.

"The doctor's said that my ankle was broken and was broken a long time ago," She explains. "I shouldn't have been playing. Sorry for the troubles," She begins to get much quieter and sounds truly sorry. She turns around and down she falls, over a bush across another bush, and then making her way (her bad ankle twisting over the wrong way) into the sticky mud puddle. "OW!" She cries.

"What's wrong?" asks Ariel, clueless.

"MY ANKLE HURTS!" Alex screams in pain. It's swelling up and I think I heard a bone crack. "FOR

REAL!" She finishes hardly able to get up. Grandpa comes when my grandma calls him and he lifts her up. She doesn't move though and neither does the ankle.

"OMG," Talia says.

"I think it's broken," Alex declares.

"You said that a minute ago," I remind her.

"That doesn't matter!"

"Alex," My grandma says her voice much more calm. "Do you think you move your ankle?" she asks.

"I'll try," Alex nods.

"Try," I whisper to Rosie's ear. "She can try," I get upset by this and turn around, unable to look. I'm upset that Alex can 'try', but she won't try for her friends. She has a reason to 'try' and move her ankle, but she needs to 'try' and stand up to Jackson.

My grandparents end up calling Alex's parents after a couple more minutes of Alex's ankle not moving. Her parents, who are always dressed in too-tight business clothes even in the summer, are furious when they learn that her ankle is hurt and grab her from my grandparents.

"That is unnecessary, Gabby," My grandma tells Alex's mom. "Jim and I are perfectly capable of making sure she is okay, you didn't need to grab her."

"Oh?" Mrs. Waters questions my grandmother, which is a bad idea to do by the way. "I don't think that you were capable because if you were then why was my daughter hurt by this no good, stupid club that she was tricked into joining? I want to know. Now." She doesn't wait for an answer, but instead pulls Alex away, who has no expression or emotion. Mr. Waters stares us all in the eye.

"Idiots," He whispers.

I stare taken aback by this. Mr. Waters has hated us and now he hates us even more since the club 'hurt his daughter'. To be honest Alex is always hurting her foot or her ankle. I don't remember when she wasn't complaining about it hurting. She can't be so hurt that she needs to quit, because we all know why she quit, but the club had nothing to do with hurting her stupid ankle. I know that's mean, but I know Alex and she wouldn't quit just because her ankle hurts.

We've got some work to do.

Rosie

I head home after practice, upset and aggravated and go up to my room to relax. This whole week has been unfair and stupid. I wish that I was better at baseball, then this never would have happened. I mean, maybe the part when Alex quit wouldn't happened, but everybody else wouldn't quit if we had won.

"Rosie you have to try," My dad told me the other night when I told him about the game and how it was all because of me. I find it hard to believe that my dad was a professional baseball player. He's so into computers and sciences now, he doesn't ever talk about when he played.

When he told me to try I nodded my head and walked away and thought about how I would try harder and would win next time. Then sadly, Alex decided to quit and turns things around. When she quit I felt betrayed. I wonder why on Earth she did that anyway.

I sit on my bed and stare at the framed picture of my mom, my dad, Sundae and I when my mom was home. Sundae is looking in the other direction barking, my dad is smiling, my mom is smiling, and

I have a look of pure happiness. I wish I always looked like that.

But now I'm stuck trying to plot a way to keep the baseball club for girls around, but it's starting to seem useless. No matter what we do nobody will want to help us out. We're hopeless.

Yesterday I almost thought about asking my old friends from the cheer and POM teams if they would join to help us out, but I backed away as soon as I thought of my new friends and how awkward and weird that would be. Nobody would be nice and it would be totally a waste of time and our time can't be wasted.

***

I wake up and have a plan of pure genius in my mind. It may not work, but that's not important right now. What's important is seeing if I can get my friends on board with this and that is all that matters.

I want to see if there's any way possible that maybe we could hold tryouts, like with the school board music video, or when we got our newbies for the team. I mean, we don't have time to let them come to us; we have to dazzle them and come to them.

I want to make this the most fun I can even if this isn't very fun right now for me. I'm cranky because I can't pitch and I'm starting to think that instead of giving up The Baseball Club, maybe I can switch my position. I can't do that yet, though. We don't have another pitcher besides me right now. I mean, Ally and Marianne used to be our backup, but since they quit we don't have anyone else.

"Tryouts?" Gwen snorts ripping a sign out of my hand. Terrified, I let her have it; the worst she can do is make fun of me for trying. "Oh, did your friends leave you? I told you they would. Sydney, I was right again they don't trust me."

Sydney jots something down on her hand.

"They didn't leave me," I assure her, although I sound unsure. Only Alex has betrayed me, Jackie and Caroline are still my best friends.

"Whatever," Gwen picks at her nails. "I want to help you." She says sounding sincere. I back away though. You never trust Gwen Biggley from just one thing she says that sounds maybe sincere. You MUST have more details.

"Why?" I ask, my questioning begins.

"Look, Rosie. I may not seem like someone who would want to help you for real, but I do and you can choose to want me or not, but I assure you if you do use my help you won't regret it." She turns away and stops, clearly awaiting my answer. I wait and listen to her go on. "I know what to do and your flyers aren't gonna help."

"What?" I give in.

"I can get you the entire POM team, the entire, cheer squad and my good friends from the dance team to play in your game on Thursday," She offers.

"No thanks," I hesitate.

"Come on!" She pleads, her eyes starting to shed tears. "All this time you've had your stupid secret club I've wanted to join." She confesses. My jaw drops. Gwen is seriously jealous of us? "It's not normal for the popular girl to not be part of a town breakthrough. I'm so proud of you guys. I know Alex hates me and Jackie could care less about me and Caroline's afraid of me and you, Rosie you were my best friend believe it or not. That short time you were nice. I never had a nice friend." She cries.

I don't say anything.

"Rosie, let me help. I know how to fix this. I will get you your team back I know how. I know how to get Alex to be your friend again too." She promises. Is Gwen Biggley the answer to our prayers?

Gwen comes over and draws out a map of our plan. She texts Sydney to forward a message to the rest of her POM and cheer teams to come to Pine Tree Park tomorrow right after school. There is where we'll discuss our plan to defeat the best team from Washers that we have to play on Thursday.

Gwen is quite good at making plans and even makes some better signs with my sparkly markers and neon pens to get people's attention. I show up at school super early to hang them up and ask Mrs. Adams if she would be willing to discuss our club with her classes. She agrees and finally I start to smile. I'm so excited.

After a while a thought dawns on me. "How are you going to make Alex come back?" I ask Gwen.

"Oh that," Her voice sounds taken aback. "I know exactly why she's not playing anymore and I have another plan, but I don't know." She stops and waits for me.

"Why don't you know?" I ask her.

"It's kind of mean, towards Jackson anyway. He's kind of the cause of all this." She explains, still confused I listen. "He was the one who tricked Alex into quitting. She didn't want to, but he knows she has a crush on him. He used her, Rosie."

Jackson Spicer, one of the nicest boys in Riverside tricked one of my best friends into quitting something she loves. I want Gwen to go through with her plan. I tell her so and she nods. You can tell that Gwen loves this.

***

I don't sit with Caroline and Jackie at lunch and quickly explain to them that Gwen is about to help us a lot. Jackie looks uncertain and Caroline looks afraid. I sit with Sydney and Gwen anyway to watch as the plan goes down.

Simply, Gwen is going to start conversation with Jackson in front of Alex, chat him up see what he's up to and then she starts the plan. She hasn't really told me what she's going to do, but I have trust that it'll work.

I sure hope so.

Gwen walks over to Jackson who's describing something to Alex who looks kind of down. Her ankle is really hurt and she has her crutches again so she always kind of is down. "Hey Jackson," Gwen says. She starts conversation and Alex glares at her. Gwen continues and starts to compliment him. I don't think she's doing the plan I think she's flirting with Jackson instead!

"So, um," Gwen cocks her head to make sure that she has Alex's attention too. "I heard you got the girl's team to break up," She says her voice mellow. "You are so bad, but good too. How'd you do it?"

My mouth drops and turns into a laugh. Alex stands up and stares openmouthed at Gwen. "You can't accuse him like that!" She screams.

"I'm not accusing," corrects Gwen. "I'm stating the facts." Jackson looks slapped and Alex shakes her head and frowns.

"Jackson thought that we were a threat," Alex says. "He had nothing to do with breaking the entire team up and Jackson likes me, right?"

"Uh," for the first time Jackson Spicer is speechless.

"Why did you do that?" Alex asks Gwen, not convinced.

"I wanted you to know that Jackson was using you. I'm your friend now," She says. "Whether you like it or not, I helped you. I helped all of you."

"Gwen Biggley is our friend?" Jackie wonders.

"Yes," I declare. "And thanks to her we have a team. We have enough people for tomorrow's game."

"Wait, we're playing in that?" Caroline freaks out. She takes off her glasses and stares blankly at everyone. "I'm so confused. I thought we gave up."

"No way," I say. "I can promise that we are going to win."

Nobody else looks fully convinced by this, I flash my best smile possible.

Alex walks away, ignoring us. I run after her, but she doesn't come back and by the time we're back in the cafeteria she's clung to Jackson's side again. I have no idea how that didn't work! She knew that Jackson used her to quit, but I don't think she was all that convinced.

Now what are we going to do for the big game tomorrow?

Alex

I walk up the bleachers and sit down next to Jackson. I can't believe the ones I thought were my friends tried to trick me into believing that Jackson would do something like that. When I ran back into the lunchroom, Jackson explained everything. He said that he only agreed to what Gwen said because he was on the spot and didn't know what she was asking. He didn't use me; he said that he really does like me and that I shouldn't believe them. They aren't worth it. So we came to watch their game and I think it's the very first time in my life I'm cheering on Washers.

Rosie's pitching this one too. She keeps trying to talk to me and make me ditch Jackson because he was in her words 'using me'. He wasn't, though and I can't believe someone like Rosie would think I would believe her over him.

Jackie's tried to get me to play, but even if I wasn't mad at him I wouldn't be able to with my stupid crutches. It was wrong to tell Miss Ruth I was quitting because of that, but now I kind of am quitting because of that and the fact that all the people playing are traders and jerks. Not worth my time.

"You cold?" asks Jackson, shivering. I nod.

Although it's much closer to summer now, it's cold. I wrap my scarf around my mouth and put on my jacket. The wind blows again and I feel relieved that I don't have to play out there today.

I don't understand why Rosie, Jackie, and Caroline didn't just give up after I quit. Instead that brought in a whole new group of girls and had Gwen Biggley lead them to this. I'd never say this to them now, but that is really inspiring. If Jackson had tricked me, but he didn't because I know him better than that, I would come back, but I don't think that I would even be able to play with my broken ankle.

I sigh and wish I was out there once I see my ex-best friends take the field. I turn to Jackson. I don't know who to believe sometimes. Maybe my friends were acting like friends and Gwen was helping and doing something in my favor. I'm so close to Jackson, I thought that he would never hurt me, but he's never liked me before I did something for him.

My heart pangs as I turn to him. I don't know what to do. Instead, I watch the baseball game to take my mind off the weird twists and turns of friendship.

Rosie warms up and misses terribly. I know she's pretty much their only pitcher right now, but they need to work with her more. She tries, but she needs to know how to pitch. I think she just throws to throw, awaiting the outcome. The outcome of this that the batter walks and Rosie starts to tear up. I wish she didn't do that every time.

I get tired after a while, because the first couple innings end up stinking and the opposing team is a bunch points ahead. I thought that I would come here rooting for Washers, but the more I see my ex-best friends I want to cheer them on.

The first base runner for us is surprisingly Gwen Biggley who runs super fast and smiles at everyone around her, even Mr. Singsang, the Washer's head coach. Mr. Singsang glares at Miss Ruth.

After Gwen, Jackie gets a base hit and the crowd is roaring. I stand up and cheer after Caroline hits a double and we score. "Yes! Go!" I shout. Jackie runs so fast around she ends up scoring too and Jackson stares nervously at me.

"I thought they would give up," He's speechless.

"No," I shake my head. "They would never do that."

"But you talked to them, didn't you? You promised you'd quit!" He's furious. I can't believe we're halfway done with the game and he just now noticed that The Baseball Club for Girls is playing and only a few runs behind!

"I quit," I say regretfully. "But they didn't and you should be ashamed." I realize where this is going. He did trick me. He knew that this day when our team would dominate would come and that he would be scared. He wanted this to never happen by tricking me and using the fact that I have a crush on him. This was the most obvious thing in the whole world and I chose not to believe my true friends. I swallow hard and regret quitting and stare angrily at my crutches and bandaged ankle. I want to show him how to hit like a girl.

"Alex!" He cries when I scoot down away from him, feeling disgusted that I let him get in the way of my friends. "You like me!"

"Yeah, no." I snap. "I don't like boys who use me. You ruined my friendship with my friends. They hate me because I quit. They thought that we had a club and now I ruined everything." I tear up and run out of words. "Bye, Jackson." I say.

"Alex!" He calls.

"Alexandria to you. I have a game to watch." I hobble off the bleachers and into the dugout.

Riverside is so state-of-the-art thanks to my parents that each dugout has a lock on the door. Yes, they have doors. I knock, almost falling off my crutches.

"Yes?" Miss Ruth asks opening the door. "Alex! You're here!" She cries, takes my crutches and shoos me in. "I know you can't play, but we need you to cheer us on." She says.

I feel so relieved as Miss Ruth assures me that I'm still part of team. "Alex!" Sydney Mister cries to the others in the dugout. I smile at them. Caroline, Rosie, and Jackie keep their distance and Gwen stands by them, her arms folded. Gwen's bag is in the spot I put mine. There is no way that dumb Gwen Biggley is replacing me. There's no way.

"Are you back in?" asks Caroline anxiously. I nod and she hugs me and Rosie and Jackie run over to hug me too. I smile and I feel so happy that my friends like me again. That's so much better than Jackson pretending to like me. I'd rather have my friends then someone who doesn't even like me.

"I'm so sorry," I say sincerely.

"Girls, hurry up!" Miss Ruth calls.

"We're down by one!" Jackie informs me. "I'm so excited, we might win!" I jump up and down along with them and instruct them to go win. Sure enough, the crowd erupts in roars again when Gwen gets another hit and Caroline's right behind her with a walk. Rosie manages to get on somehow and Jackie hits them in. I find that Talia and Ariel aren't useless. Ariel groundouts, but advances Rosie and Talia ends up getting on. I scream loud and annoy Mr. Singsang who looks like he's had enough.

"What is going on?" He demands to know. "What is this? Is this even a team?" I laugh and nod at him. Miss Ruth explains that we are The Baseball Club for Girls and we are truly amazing. "Whatever," he snorts.

"GO GET 'EM!" I scream louder to my friends. They turn around and flash a huge smile at me, all of them. I wish I was out there, but watching them win is just as good as winning myself. I cheer louder and louder until my throat is sore and it's not a one run game anymore. We are winning.

When Rosie goes out there to pitch again and walks someone I start to panic. If Rosie can't pitch well then it's simple. Washers wins. We lose, it's so easy to lose and not fair. I bet they are feeling the same way every time we score a run.

Rosie throws a strike, and then another, and then right before my eyes is Rosie Ann Dawkins' first ever strikeout. She does a mini dance on the mound and starts to giggle so loud I can hear her from the dugout.

This has to be our best game.

Once they come in the last inning begins and I start to feel jittery. We could win this, our first win is in our hands, we have to reach for it and try.

"You guys can do this," I assure them. Gwen looks at me uncertain.

"I'm sorry," She apologizes.

"For what?" I ask confused.

"I'm sorry," She says again. "Alex, you know the other day at school I didn't mean to pull you away from Jackson, I wanted to help and I guess because you hate me you didn't trust me." She pauses. "Remember in the hallway that day when he asked you to quit? I knew he was going to do that, and I shot you that grin because I wanted you to catch on. I did, Alex. I wasn't trying to sabotage you."

"Okay," I say emotionless. Gwen can apologize, but that doesn't mean she's my friend.

"I'm not sorry for those other things, though." She snaps, correcting herself. "We aren't friends, you know that, right?"

"I know," I nod and laugh. She turns away. I don't want to be friends with snotty Gwen, but I'm happy that she's at least sorry for something she did that made me mad. "Now go and show the Washers team who is boss." They line up and get ready. I smile.

With one final hit from Rosie we win the game. The Washers are miserable and walk away as sore losers while we jump around and celebrate. Miss Ruth and Mr. Jim promise to take us to Pizza Township for a little party and dinner and we happily go.

As I have my friends assist me walk with my crutches I see Jackson waiting beside the dugout. I shoot my friends a glance and sigh.

"Alex," he starts.

"Are you apologizing?" I ask him nicely.

"Uh, I was gonna say that I'm sorry and I shouldn't have used you to quit, you guys, well girls, really are good." He says. "Please accept my apology."

"Okay," I reply. "I accept your apology."

"Are you quitting?"

"No!" I cry. "You can't apologize and then ask that, Jackson. I'm sorry, but I'm not quitting."

And we walk away.

Jackson can wait until he finds out how to apologize to someone the right way.

Caroline

I cry into my tissue and put on my dress shoes. I don't want to go to the stupid award ceremony. I already know the outcome. We lost so many games that there's no possible way that we're going to the postseason. I cry into my tissue again. My mom said that she can hardly believe that I made it to where I am now and that she's extremely proud. My dad said the same and they are both coming with me to our awards ceremony.

I don't know who's going to the postseason, but I know that I want to. I want to so bad and it's out of the question. The top three teams that have the most wins end up going to the postseason along with one wildcard team that Mr. Waters, being head of the Riverside Waters Athletic Association, gets to pick. I know he'd never pick us, he didn't want us to play in the first place why would he want us to go to the end and try to win? He wouldn't which is why I'm upset. I think we proved something. Something that if it wasn't for us wouldn't have ever been done.

I sigh once more and follow my parents and siblings into our minivan. I'm not ready to find out which teams won.

"Don't worry too much," Cece says, slapping my thigh. "You're so going to win wildcard. Trust me." For the first time Cece is actually missing one of her big school activities to go to my awards ceremony.

I run towards Rosie, Alex, and Jackie as soon as we arrive and sit down. My heart starts thumping and I force myself to smile. "I'm nervous," I mumble.

Miss Ruth and Mr. Jim shush us and make us be quiet so that we can hear when they begin. I stare at the big stage. We're in the theater part of the Riverside Waters Athletic Association and they have this really giant stage that they use for awards ceremonies and plays and such. They have nice and cozy seats as well.

"Attention!" Mr. Waters appears on stage and talks into the microphone. His team, having the most wins, is sitting in the front row. "I'd like to begin with our baseball season awards, then move on to hockey and our cheer awards, thank you."

I look around the back of the auditorium to find my parents and siblings. I don't see them, I cross my fingers nervously. I want to win the wildcard. I want to win the wildcard.

Some teams are called up to the stage and the coaches award them with pins and give short speeches. Miss Ruth and Mr. Jim go behind the curtain and come out to hand out our awards.

"Can we have The Baseball Club for Girls?" Mr. Waters taps his foot and rolls his eyes. Miss Ruth hands us our pins and Mr. Jim gives me a certificate. When I'm back at my seat I put the pin on and smile. They made us pink and purple pins.

"First Place, Riverside Waters Dolphins!" Mr. Waters announces into the microphone. The Dolphins cheer and scream and take their trophies to back to their seats. I knew we would never win that one.

"Second Place, Washers Warriors!" The Washers boys cheer and hold up their second place trophies to the crowd. First place trophies are blue and the second place trophies are silver.

Third place goes to some other team and their trophies are black. I wait, starting to sweat like crazy, anxiously for the wildcard team. Wildcard trophies are tiny and not the most rewarding, but they would be very rewarding for us. So rewarding.

"Our wildcard team is usually a team with the fourth most wins, but I talked with some head coaches and we found that this team deserved it more than a fourth place team. Congratulations to…"

"The Baseball Club for Girls!"

I get up and scream my head off running to get my trophy. Sure enough, the trophies are bright pink and say our names on them. I grab mine from Miss Ruth and clutch it closely to my heart. I have no idea why I had such doubts about us. We are going to the postseason! The postseason! I would never imagine playing for our athletic association and making a difference.

"I would like to say that I know that these girls are absolutely amazing and talented." Miss Ruth says, choking up. "I want you to know that we will be back next year with more girls who want to play. Congrats, girls, you deserve this!" I hold up my trophy in totally awe. I'm so thrilled. I can't believe this.

"I knew you could do it!" My mom calls running towards me. She gives me a big hug and my dad comes in too.

"You are amazing," He says.

"What did I tell you?" asks Cece. "I knew it!" Ashley and Cody beg to know what happened and I explain that I won. They hug me tight and ask to see my trophy.

"No fair!" Ashley cries. "Pink! I want a pink trophy!"

"They should have green trophies," Cody suggests.

"Caroline, I am so proud of you," My dad says. "I might sign up to announce one of your games."

"Thanks, Dad." I hug him.

"WE WON!" my friends shout in my ear. I laugh and we discuss our postseason plans. Rosie suggests that we wear these things called high heeled cleats; I guess they're high heels only in cleat form. "They're real," Rosie insists.

And that was how The Baseball Club for Girls came to be.

Dedicated to My Family

~ Author's Note ~

The Postseason! Yay! The Baseball Club has proven they could win. Did you think that they could? What else can I say? This book was so fun to write and I hope that everyone enjoyed it.

I wrote this book because I love to play softball and watch baseball with my dad. I thought that writing a book where girls had to try and prove that they too can play a sport and be good at it! Riverside Waters didn't have that and now thanks to Caroline, Alex, Rosie, and Jackie they do. I think these girls are inspirational to anyone who says they can't.

Here are some cool facts and my take on the book itself. I know you want to hear that ☺

What is Riverside Waters?
Riverside Waters is the town the girls all live in. It is mainly referred to as 'Riverside' because Waters is Alex's family's last name. Alex's family (as in the book) kind of owns Riverside and owns business and parks (like Pine Tree Park).

Why doesn't Riverside Waters have any girl's sports?
Riverside Waters has the basics cheer, POM, and

dance for girls, but not any football or baseball for the girls because Mr. Water's great-grandparents built the town and didn't think that girls would want to play. I know I don't mention this in the book, but in the book it is pretty well stated. They don't have sports because they don't and never did and that's the end of it according to Mr. Waters.

What happened with Jackson and Alex?
The Jackson and Alex concept can be tricky with some people. Jackson, being popular and on the Riverside baseball team, can be easily crushable. Alex had a crush on him, of course and when he started talking to her he was all for her club. In fact, I think he liked her too, but when Alex kind of showed him that she was good her got worried and used her to his advantage and made her quit so he didn't have to worry about them ever beating him. He was satisfied, until Gwen spoiled his plan and was okay again when Alex didn't believe her. Alex thought it over and realized that her friends were looking out for her and she told Jackson that she knew he tricked her and didn't you read the book? You should know. Anyway, he basically tricked her into thinking he liked her too and begged her to quit.

Gwen: Nice or Naughty?
Gwen is probably the character that changed the

most as the story progressed. She became nicer in some ways and meaner in some. She didn't want to watch Caroline, Alex, Rosie, and Jackie fail. She did apologize to Alex, but didn't exactly say sorry for everything she did. I'd say that Gwen is nice and naughty.

What happens in the postseason?
Well, that answer is in the second book coming soon!

I would like to thank a number of people who inspired me and helped me write this book!

My daddy and mommy: They inspire me all the time and I love, love, love them. Rosie wouldn't have a baseball connection if it wasn't for my daddy. I'm so happy they both want to read this or else I wouldn't have anyone to read this for me! Thank you so much! I love you, Mommy and Daddy!

My Brothers: Nick, Noah, and Andrew you annoy me sometimes, but I love you too! So much! Are you guys gonna read this book? Please!

Tiger Puppy: I love my puppy!

My Family! : Grandma, Grandpa, Aunt Sarah, Uncle Jeff, Aunt Natalie, Uncle Jay, Charley,

Grandma Kay, Aunt Karen, and more! You guys inspire me so much! I love you!

Ms. Grech – Thank you for supporting me and helping me so much!

My Best Friends: My friends! They are amazing and inspiring and we can have a book swap with the other books! Do you like my book? Dominic, Juliet, Meghann, Julia, and more!

Thank you readers ☺

Emily J. Proctor

About the Author

Emily J. Proctor

Emily J. Proctor wrote The Baseball Club for Girls. Emily loves to sing, act, write, and read. She also enjoys watching baseball with her dad. She has three brothers and a puppy who is so cute! She has written other books such as *The Story of my Life* and *Anna and the Magical Fairies* when she was only seven! She's working on the sequel to *The Baseball Club for Girls!* She hopes you enjoyed her book as much as she enjoyed writing it!

Made in the USA
Charleston, SC
24 January 2012